Amazon Lost

Amazon Lost

Regina Ann Penn

YOU'RE NOT SLEEPING TONIGHT!

RAW Books Publishing™

Published by RAW Books Publishing™

Copyright 2015 by Regina Ann Penn

First Edition

Book design by Roger A. Wilson

Cover by Jake Clark

ISBN-10: 0692451471
ISBN-13: 978-0692451472
ASIN: B00Z7Y8UM4

10 9 8 7 6 5 4 3 2 1

Dedicated to Fernando.
You are my inspiration.

Chapter 1

I was soaked. I hadn't been in such a downpour for a long time. Most people have enough sense to stay inside during a tropical storm, but sometimes duty gets the better of my senses. I always relished such times though. The exertion of running through the forest was fantastic, and doubly so in the rain. It just seemed so...naughty, like it was something you weren't supposed to do, even when you had to. Nobody would have thought it of me in those days, but doing the unexpected was such a great turn on. That was the thing about taboo - knowing what you should not do, but you do it anyway.

The rain felt good, like bathing, but not in the pond. Running in the open air, it felt like streaking naked alone knowing at any time someone could spy you. Oh! If I could have been naked. I thought about it, and it made me wet. Well, wetter. But now wasn't the right time. As I said, duty.

Rain water is good for your hair too. It keeps it healthy, and that's important. To me at least. I didn't really care what the other girls did with their hair. I love long hair, but I had to keep it short. Couldn't have had it snagging on branches while hunting in the woods. I had to keep up appearances. At least my short hair was soft, not like dried grass. Like Emere's hair.

It was a dark night, especially away from the lights of the village, so it was hard to see through the thick trees and falling rain. That made my sisters all but invisible as they ran with me. I could hear them easier than see them. They sounded like a herd of deer even over the heavy rain patter. It was just hunters like me that trained to be silent in the forest, and since there were few of us among the group that night, I knew right were each of my sisters was by sound alone.

It annoyed me how much faster they ran than I could though, and it always had been like that. It didn't make it any easier to accept. I couldn't run down a deer like some of them could, but it wasn't like I was slow. They were just much faster because their bodies were augmented in ways mine wouldn't allow. I reacted faster than anyone else, able to catch something dropped off a table before hitting the ground, but that was my only claim of fame with body magic. However, I could've claimed

2

infamy, but I wouldn't let anybody know that secret.

I smelled smoke. It amazed me that something could be burning in that rain. It did explain why things were getting brighter as the trees thinned near the beach though. When I finally left the trees and stepped on the beach, I could see my sisters waiting at the tree line.

We surveyed the scene and saw fire everywhere. The beach was on fire. The rocks off shore were on fire. The water was on fire too. A ship had capsized on the rocks and was burning. All of that in spite of the rain. I felt the heat even at the tree line. This was going to be hot, and not how I usually liked it.

The ship was the largest man-made thing I'd ever seen. I now know it wasn't that big, but it was huge to me at the time. It was a charter fishing ship that was carrying some cargo, and a lot of that had fallen off. Some crates were floating in the water, and some had washed up on the beach. I'm sure most of it just sank, and though the rocks were not far out, the ocean was already deep there, so any that sank were lost to us. We would try to save those that floated, but they weren't our first worry. That was the survivors. Life came before treasures, even of strangers.

One of the Blessed joined us on the beach to coordinate the efforts. She was newly pregnant and was not showing yet, which was why she had come and not one of the others. We gathered around her as she starting giving assignments. My sisters were sent up beach and down, looking for survivors first and usable treasures second, like always.

When she got to me, I offered, "I'll swim out to the rocks." It was dangerous to do, and most would try to avoid that task, especially with the fire on the water. It could wash over to you more quickly than you could swim away from it. If caught, you had to submerge and try to swim beyond the flaming edge. Girls have drowned from that, and burned. But I had something to prove. I wasn't as fast as the others, but I was the bravest of them. I would go where they were too afraid to go. I would be a hero and save anyone stuck on the rocks from the shipwreck.

"I should go," another girl said. "I'm a much stronger swimmer than Asoese."

I glared at her. It was Emere. It was always Emere. She didn't look at me, but I saw the smile on her lips. How dare she think she could...?

"I agree. Emere, get out there. Asoese, work the beach here. There's a lot of debris to dig through."

Emere turned to me and held up her hands to show off. I watched the skin between her fingers grow, creating a membrane between them like flippers. I knew her toes were doing the same thing, but I didn't look down at them. I hated her for that. Not only

4

was I the slowest in the tribe, but some like Emere could change their bodies in some way. She couldn't turn her arm or leg into stone like some other sisters, but she could grow the webbing. She could even grow spikes off of her hands, elbows, and knees. I wished I could've shown off. But I wouldn't.

"Really," Emere said, "only the best should swim to the rocks. Working the beach is good for people like you. Bye!" She ran off, waving back at me, showing off her webbing even more.

"What a cunt!" I cussed.

I was left to work the beach. Anybody could work the beach. But I had to do what the tribe needed. Pride never before tribe. That was one of our biggest tenants. Tribe always came first. Selfishness killed. So I got to work, thinking that with any luck Emere would get caught in the fire. Not that I wanted her to get burnt, but if her hair got singed off, I would probably giggle at that. Not in public, because that would be horrible of me. In private, I would laugh my ass off thinking about her bald head!

The white sands glowed orange from the flickering fire light. Wreckage from small bits of castoff debris to large chunks of ship was scattered across the beach, many of which were already beginning to get buried by the sand. There were a few visible bodies among it all, and other girls were checking on them, trying to find survivors. A few moved, but none seemed in good shape.

They were collapsed on the sand either from exhaustion or injuries.

I hurried over to a section of beach none of the other girls seemed to be worrying about. There was a big chunk of boat there with only a couple small fires around it. It was just enough to provide light but not be a danger. The boat piece was outer hull on one side, white and smooth and reflecting firelight off of the wet surface. I stepped around it. The edges of the white bit was torn, silver metal that looked like a giant ripped it free and tossed it on the beach. The rest of the discarded chunk was an indiscernible, non-geometric bit of ship hull.

I barely heard a sound over the raining and breaking waves. It was a whimpering carried on quick, panicked breaths. It sounded like a girl, a frightened girl. I couldn't see her, so I continued to circle around the wreckage. Looking into it, I expected to see her trapped inside.

"Hello? I'm here to help," I said.

She did not reply. I only heard the whimpering continue.

Then I saw her. Part of her, at least. It was only her hand, sticking out from under the massive thing. I got down on my knees and began pulling the sand from around the hand, piling it up into my lap. I kept digging, trying to make a hole around her to pull her through from under the debris.

6

When I touched her hand, it starting to spasm, and she grasped for me in panic. The whimpering stopped as she called out, "Is somebody there? Help me! I'm trapped." It was barely audible, coming muffled as her face was probably pushed into the sand. I'm sure she could barely breathe under there.

I worked fast. I imagined how terrifying it would be to be trapped under that thing with its weight pushing down, trying to crush me. I worked frantically, shoveling the sand out of the ever increasing hole. Sand is not a good medium to dig in as it does not keep its shape well, especially in the rain. The sides kept falling into the hole, making it difficult to progress quickly.

As I dug deeper, a second hand emerged. I noticed her fingernails had been painted red. I was mesmerized by this. We had makeup like that, but we couldn't create such vivid color. I began to think of this woman as my little princess that I had to save, who would reward me with a kiss.

With her second hand free, she tried to help dig as well, but it was only her wrists that were out, giving her very little range of motion. Her hands desperately flapped about, accomplishing nothing but churning my stomach. The motion seemed so inhuman. Hands and wrists don't normally move like that, looking much more insect-like, jerky in motion.

I stopped trying to dig deeper and followed her arms,

digging back underneath the wreckage. It was then I found it.

It was a black box. It didn't look like much. It was the size of my hand with a black cord rising up from the top. Numbered buttons were on the front, and a glowing screen was above those. The screen was cracked though, so I couldn't read anything on it. It was just a glow behind spider webbing. I sat it down beside me. I had never seen one before, but I know what it was. My heart raced having found it. It was another taboo. But a real one. I smiled as I kept digging.

I passed her elbows and found the top of her head. She was blond. I lay down to extend my arms farther in. I cleared the sand out from in front of her face, and she took a deep, gasping breath. I know, it was horrible for me to think at that time with her life on the line, but I couldn't help but reflect on how pretty she was.

I smiled at her. Her face returned a look of horror. I saw it in her eyes. I remember them clearly still, like I could take out a picture of her anytime I wished. She knew, just knew, she was going to die, but she wasn't going to go out whimpering. She fought.

She was able to move sand from around herself now, and she worked like a shovel, pushing the sand away. We worked together and cleared much of what was trapping her. I turned and

8

planted my feet against the wreckage, reached back through my legs, and grasped her hands.

I pulled. She did not budge. We went back to digging again, opening a hole under her torso frantically. She leaned down into the hole as it widened, and I tried to pull again. This time, she slid an inch. Only her legs were still stuck, so I braced myself again and pulled harder. She came forward a couple more inches for my efforts.

"Just keep breathing," I told her, just as much as I told myself.

I pulled again, and her hips fell into the hole. Her shorts had come off, left behind buried in the sand. She wiggled and kicked herself free as I kept pulling. She slid out of the hole and stood up. We looked at each other for a breathless moment from the exertion. We felt joy, disbelief, fright, anger. Everything. It was the raw emotion of life that filled us. We grabbed each other in an embrace, and we both cried. It was like we were long lost friends whose company we missed as if it was our own heartbeat, but we obviously knew nothing about each other.

The wreckage then shifted, falling forward into the hole. We jumped to the side and shrieked in fright. It came to rest and both of us were mostly unharmed.

I saw the radio half buried in the sand next to the debris. I kicked more sand over it to cover it up. It was mine. I would be back.

I turned back to the girl. She was pretty. And so pale. Everyone on the island was dark from the sun tanning our skin, but even the babies were darker than her. She looked so exotic. She was almost as white as milk, like the sun had never kissed her skin. But I sure wanted to.

I couldn't help but looking down. She didn't have any pubes. It was confusing then because she obviously had become a woman as she had an ample chest. We didn't bother shaving ourselves on the island. That never even crossed my mind. She noticed my gaze then and embarrassingly covered herself with her hands, now completely conscious of her half naked state.

"Come on. We need to get you to the others."

She did not say anything as I led her backs to the tree line. A small group of survivors was gathering as the girls brought them to the Blessed.

"Gina!" a woman yelled. She rushed over to me and the girl.

"Oh, Mom!" My princess hugged her back. "Where's Dad?"

"I'm here," a man called. I'm sure he would have come over as well, but he was tied up to the other men. The two girls looked at him. I'm sure it was strange to them that he had been tied up, but that was just what we did when these things happened.

Most of the survivors looked similar. I'm not saying they were all as pretty as my princess, but their skin was so pale. Most of them anyway, as a couple were darker than even us. It was weird to see that back then. I didn't know skin could look so different. There was a great difference in the tribe already, but just not so stark, like milky white faces to charcoal black. And they all were so afraid.

What I found really surprising were the men. They looked me in the face, so bold they were. That I did not like, but they would soon learn manners. For their sakes.

"I got one!" Emere shouted as she came up. She was leading another man she probably saved from out by the rocks. I couldn't help but smirk. I saved a woman. She saved a man. How useless.

In the end, there were a handful of survivors, both men and women. Some children. We began to lead them back to the village then, leaving the beach and their old lives behind.

Chapter 2

Soaked from the rain and pumped up by the adrenaline of saving that girl, I barely kept my skirt and wrap on until I was home. The skirt was made of a soft and flexible tree bark that wrapped around my waist and tied together. The top was made from cloth scavenged from wreckages. These tended to be the most colorful clothes on the island as the bark usually was muted. The wrap went from my back to cross in front and cup my boobs with the ends going over my shoulders to tie behind my neck.

I peeled off the wet clothes immediately when out of the downpour, before I even had the curtain pulled back over the door. I stretched happily in the warmth of my hut, bare ass naked and freezing cold. Wood popped in the fireplace, and my bed covered in soft furs greeted my gooseflesh when I fell on it. I stretched, letting out a little moan against my desire as I warmed.

It was then I looked around my hut. "Hi, sweetie," I cooed.

The well-muscled man in my room turned and looked at me. He wore a simple loin skin, showing off his muscles and tanned body. He turned back away and finished folding a blanket before gathering up the food dishes from earlier in the day. I loved coming home and having that stuff taken care of. He was the best.

"I need your gentle caressing," I moaned. "Come and get me."

He stood with the dishes and hurried out of the hut, heading into the rain. I watched him go.

I sighed happily and rolled onto my belly, my breasts falling to the side and squishing under me. I loved the feel of the fur on my naked body as my goose bumps relaxed away, especially as it rubbed against my nipples. They were already stone hard from the cold, hard enough to hurt, to ache, and brushing the fur sent electricity dancing over my chest and between my legs.

"Sweetie!" I called out again.

Lelei, my lovely flower. It was always a good day when I came home to her. That always made me giggle when I said it to her, but she didn't find it so amazing. You see, my name meant "different day," and hers was "good." So together we were a good day. It's the small joys in life really.

She was a beauty. A curvy woman with a slight swelling of a belly that I loved, and cheeks that did not dimple in but slightly curved out. Everything about her was curvy, like any real woman. Some called her fat, but that was just so unfair. She was amazingly hot! I could run my hands over her body all night, and I had before, and I intended to that night as well.

Her best feature had to be her hair though. I love good hair, but hers was unique. Lelei had blood from a survivor in her. Her mother had freckles and red hair. She gained that disposition as well, having fire red hair as soft as anything I've ever known on her head and upon her musky womanhood.

"How did it go?" she asked.

She was frustratingly fully clothed. I grunted at that as I waved her forward, beckoning her closer. I started to untie her skirt.

"Some good and some bad," I replied.

"So you saved someone but Emere got the best of you."

My hands stopped moving at that. I stared at her hard, my jaw slack in feigned indignation. "How could you think Emere could get the best of me?"

"Well, you know, your best is not all that good really," she replied playfully. "I suppose I've been pleasantly surprised by you

14

occasionally."

"You're cruel." I rolled on my back after her skirt fell away, allowing her eyes to trail over my body, which they did. "At least let me tell the story instead of you always knowing about it. I like telling stories."

"Yeah, but I already told you you really are not that good."

"You might as well stab me with a knife," I said.

Lelei sat on the bed in front of me, sitting back on her legs with her calves under her. "I'm ready for your stunning story of heroics. I'm sure you'll be made queen of the island by the time everyone hears this story."

"Don't kid," I replied, nervously. "We haven't had queens for more than a few generations, and they were not..."

Lelei stood back up and put her hands on her hips. "I know all that. Stop talking to me like I don't know things. I've heard the stories too."

"Sorry, sweetie," I said, chastised.

"So what happened with Emere?"

"I was going to swim out to the rocks."

Lelei came back down on her knees again more out of shock than anything else. "You were going to do what? And I thought you were one of the smarter girls."

"Hey, now! I work hard on those stories going around

about me. It's the only way I can get any respect. I needed to make a good story."

She looked at me crossly. "You could just get pregnant and solve that problem. You would be Blessed then."

"I'm not doing that," I grumbled. "I'm not taking a man's seed. That's just gross."

"That's the sacrifice to get power. Bear children for the tribe and govern while pregnant. Your mother..."

"Do we have to talk about her?"

Lelei sat back down. "No." She looked away.

We have had that argument many times before. She didn't want to get pregnant either, but I was the one with ambition. Like my mother, I have to admit, but I wasn't willing to do just anything for the respect. A woman should not be degraded as a baby making machine, even for the good of the tribe. How many sisters did I have? I don't really know. My mother was almost always pregnant since she first bled.

"Anyway," I said, trying to get the conversation back to how much of a hero I was. If the conversation did not change, there was going to be no sexy time, and that was not an option. "Emere was chosen to go because of her horrible fingers and toes. That webbing is just gross."

Lelei rolled her eyes at me, knowing I was jealous. Not that

I would admit it though.

"I ended up digging a girl out of the sand who was pinned under a ton of rubble that was on fire. I saved her life."

"Well then, you are a hero." Lelei clapped her hands in mock delight. She was playing, but I enjoyed it. "You deserve a reward then."

"Yes, I do!"

Lelei leaned down and kissed me, her nose touching my chin and mine on her's. It's a weird thing, kissing someone upside down. I'd been kissing her for a few months, a record for me really, so I was used to the feel of her lips. Upside down made it feel like it was someone else entirely. That was exciting, so much that it caught my breath. When she pulled away, I released my baited breath with a sigh.

Her smile was lewd when she leaned back down, showing her naughty intentions. She did not go for my lips. Oh no. Her lips found the side of my neck. She kissed me. My goose bumps came rushing back. She closed her lips on my flesh again and brushed her teeth against me. I shuddered and drew in a deep breath, trying to keep myself calm. That deep breath was full of her scent. That did not help.

Lelei's lips went searching, kissing from one side of my neck to the other. And then she began to move down, nipping at my collar bone.

I squealed. "Not fair!"

Lelei smiled, stopping her unrelenting lips as they pulled tight, and a giggle escaped her serious composure. Her tongue touched the base of my neck, giving me shivers again. She traced a line downward with her tongue, and it flicked at one of my erect nipples. I felt that on the bottoms of my feet, and along my calf muscles.

Her hand cupped my left breast, and her lips closed on my right nipple. She sucked lightly and swirled her tongue around its tenderness. Her other hand caressed and kneaded my other boob. I was not going to lay there and take that with her chest hanging above my face. They were smaller than mine, and her nipples lighter. I arched my head back and stuck out my tongue and licked her peaks.

She shrieked in surprise to my great delight, and an evil laugh flowed from me. "Muahahaha."

It was then she bit, hard. I gasped, but the bite did not last long. Her mouth moved to my left side to give the first nipple a much needed reprieve. Her tongue got to work again, licking in smaller and smaller circles, closing in on the hard nipple. Then she touched the areola, and her lips closed upon it. Oh, it was heaven.

I dared to touch her's again with my tongue, but she

18

twisted her body, pulling the puckering flesh from my mouth. She lowered and smacked my face with them back and forth before pressing them down. I was smothered in her chest. I pushed them together in my face and shook my head back and forth.

And then they were gone, pulled away. She stretched across me, kissing as she went. Down the middle of my stomach, she kissed my navel but did not stay there. Her lips moved down farther, all the while her hips came floated above me. I grabbed the sides of them with my hands and squeezed slightly.

So slowly. So teasingly. Her leg, bent at the knee, came up beside my head and extended a little past my shoulder. Lelei paused moving then, and I felt something. It was wet. It was rough, and it caressed down the side of my bottom lips. I shuddered, and the gooseflesh came back with vengeance down my whole right side. Her tongue licked down the other side, and the goose bumps attacked that side of my body as well.

Her hand caressed me gently, running her fingernails along the skin of the outside of my flower. Her hand laid flat against me and pushed down. Her fingers spreading, pulling my wanting lips apart, exposing my sex. Lelei leaned down, and her tongue flicked at my clit. Energy arched all over my body as my need peaked.

I wanted her and nothing else. I needed her touch like nothing else. I desired her tongue. I wanted her fingers inside me.

I swelled at the idea. But I also needed her velvet lips from between her legs. I pulled on her hips, and she brought her other leg up.

Her muff of red hair hovered over my face. I could smell her musk as she grew wetter with her own need. I raised my right arm over my head, making sure it would not be trapped under her. I ran my fingers between her lips, nudging the folds of tender flesh aside, exposing her pink little nub.

It was hard to focus on what I was doing with her head between my spread legs. I didn't even really know what she was doing to me, but my body absolutely approved. My breath was coming in short gasps as my tongue flicked to her clit, returning the favor of quelling my need.

She gasped, and I felt her breath blow over me. Relentlessly, my tongue flicked over and over her little pink pearl. But it was not enough. I needed more! I pushed my face in there, locking my lips around her nub and sucked as my tongue caressed it.

Moans, loud moans, escaped her throat then. Her body pressed down against mine, her breasts on my belly and mine on hers. She shuddered as pleasure racked her body. But I was just getting started. My free hand was for more than just spreading her open to my attack. My index and ring fingers began to rub at her opening. She no longer moaned. Lelei now screamed out in her pleasure and desire.

I pressed my fingers inside, and her muscles fought against them, trying to push the invaders out. I did not let them. I pushed in harder, moving my whole arm in rhythm, sliding in and out of her. The faster I moved, the moister she became. I heard her fluids smacking with my fingers in their assault of her, though it was a little hard to hear it over the moans.

She had not stopped her work on me during this, and I too was shouting as the pleasure rolled through me uncontrollably. I spread my legs farther and rolled my hips up to her, to give her a better angle, serving myself up like a platter of fruit.

Her fingers spread me open as she pushed inside, rubbing against the walls of my vagina. Lelei curved her fingers up, putting pressure behind my pubic bone. I felt like I had to pee suddenly, and that was a good thing. She always knew how to find my spot.

She pounded her hand against me, her fingers moving in and out, hitting that special place with each thrust. My muscles across my whole body began to tense as energy swelled inside me. I kept getting wetter, but I didn't want it to happen yet. I fought it down. She was not going to get off so easily. I knew her just as well as she knew me. I curved my fingers inside her as well. Instantly, I felt her body tense up. The race was on!

Or so I thought it was. She cheated then. Her ring finger began to rub against my puckered backside. Attacked on all three sides, it was all over. She was vigorous, pounding me hard and quick, and licking my nub. The tension built to its peak, and it flowed over. My muscles twitched, clenching in intense release. My mind went blank, lost in a forest of pleasure.

Then Lelei was lying next to me, her arm wrapped around me. She held me tightly, like she was afraid I would vanish.

I asked her, "Did you...?"

"Oh yeah," she said, smiling. "Right after you." She sighed contently.

We were both breathing hard and covered in sweat. And I felt glorious.

Chapter 3

Lying on the pile of fur that was my bed, I looked at a paw of a large cat. The claws were nearly as long as my fingers and the pads were larger than my palm. The fur was glossy and soft, colored black with barely visible circles. This was the paw of an apex predator, a cat in its prime of power. This was the raw fury of the animal kingdom.

These cats weren't normally spotted on the island. Some said they had seen one from time to time, but nobody had ever brought one back to the village from a hunt. Most thought they weren't alive on the island anymore. They're probably only stories some of the girls tell, or just a shadow half seen through the trees. Mistaken identity.

The leather flap of my hut was pulled open. My eyes went large in surprise, and I hid the paw under the furs. That was for me and nobody else. It was then I remembered I was naked. I tried to cover up by grabbing furs and rolling to pull them on top of me.

It was Lelei. She held a hand over her mouth and was trying not to laugh.

I scowled at her. "That's no fair!"

"But it's so funny. Besides, I didn't think you were so ashamed about your butt. It was glowing at me like the rising Sun."

"Har, har."

"It's time to get up," Lelei said. "Unless you want me to come join you?"

"Well now, if you're offering?" I let the thought trail off.

"Why not? It's not like we would be missing anything important, like the Blessed meeting about the survivors in the next few moments."

At that, I was standing on the bed, ready to pounce to the pile of my clothes. I tore into them, getting myself presentable. Lelei was still standing in the doorway, smirking at me as she waited.

"Let's go," I said as I walked past her. "Stop trying to hold me up."

24

She turned and followed me, still smiling.

The village was designed in rings. In the middle was a ring of rocks with a couple logs on the west side for the Blessed to sit on, facing the rising of Mother Sun. Outside of that ring were the first circle of huts. These were the birthing huts and wet-nurse houses. The next ring was for the elders. They did not run the tribe, as only the pregnant woman were given that responsibility, but they were respected for their wisdom and contribution to all of us through their lives. Every one of them could no longer bare children, as the change was what made a woman an elder.

Next were artisan huts. Here were our cooks, weavers, shoe makers, and the medicine woman. Farther out were the huts of everyone else. It didn't matter where you lived. It only mattered where the vacant hut was to move into. We didn't build new huts as the tribe never grew larger but seemed to maintain its population despite the new babies that always seemed to come. Past those huts were the men's. They were larger but functioned as nothing more than sleeping spaces. They had too much work to do each day to spend any time leisurely, so their huts were merely for sleeping.

Lelei and I went to the rock circle in the center of the tribe. The Blessed were already seated on their log, and the women rescued last night were standing in front of them, facing away from our Mother Sun. Sitting behind them were the men. A spread of food was placed on mats behind them. Anyone was allowed to partake, even these men who were not yet told their proper place. The survivors were all eating. They seemed starved.

Most men who came to us had a lot to learn about their role in the world. I couldn't imagine how backwards the rest of the world was with how most of the new men acted after arriving. They tried to make demands of us usually. Some became physical. A couple even had tried to tell us they were a god and we should worship them. It was almost like they thought having a dick was a super power. They were so absurd. The men and their dicks both!

My mother stood up from among the Blessed. She was their unofficial speaker. I have been told that was not a normal thing, but she got that honor purely by the sheer number of years of serving in the Blessed.

"As we gather here, we offer praise to the Sun." She held her hands up to the sky, the rising sun's brightness reflected on her swollen belly. "Praise that our answers are wise and just. Praise that our plants grow strong. Praise that our roots remain firm. Praise that we will weather this storm."

"Blessed is the Sun in Her glory. She brings life in Her light and peace in Her shade," the gathered women chanted together. It was the normal sort of thing we said.

"Judgment has been passed before the light of the Sun, and we see the Sun has risen to bless these convictions."

The survivors, at the word of "convictions," got noticeably upset. They began to fidget, and scared and outraged voices called out. My mother raised her hands to silence and still them. They grew quiet again, but their eyes showed dismay as they watched her.

She continued, "The women, survivors of the storm brought to our shores, will be allowed entrance to the tribe through the Right of Passage."

"But what about going home?" one of the survivor women asked.

My mother smiled at her, in a...well, motherly smile. It was the first time I saw one of those on her. It was disconcerting. I thought she was going to eat that woman after smothering her with a pillow while she slept like a baby. My imagination was pretty vivid in those days, but my mother was ruthless in all things. I was also pretty sure that was not far from the truth of what went through her head at first.

What she said was, "You, all of you, will call this island home, this village home, and the women here your sisters. There is no going elsewhere. Once you are brought here, there is nothing else, only what the sea and the Sun bring us."

"But what about our families and jobs? We have lives back home," the survivor asked.

"The world will continue on without you, just as you will continue on without it."

"But we need...."

"No," my mother said, all motherly tones gone. She sounded like a jungle cat screeching in the night. "There is nothing left for you out there. The world will think you are dead. If you leave, you would risk the tribe. We will not allow your selfish desires to harm the tribe. You will become one of us, and that means you must live by Tribe over Pride. Your lives are meaningless, but as a part of the tribe, you will have meaning."

"What is the Right of Passage?" a different survivor asked as the first one sat down.

My mother answered, "It is the ritual that will secure your place with us as an adult. You are merely children in the eyes of the tribe before that. You have no voice and no rights as a child until you become an adult among us. You have no say in your choices. You cannot take your own hut. You cannot have a child."

"And what of the men?" another woman asked. She was the mother of Gina, the teenage girl I saved last night. "You said the women will be offered a place with you. What of the men?"

"What is your concern about them?" my mother asked.

28

Her tone was beginning to sound dangerous.

"I want to know what will happen with my husband."

There was a gasp through the crowd. I know this may seem hard to understand, but in the tribe, men were not allowed personhood. They were our servants, no better than sheep.

My mother answered, "I am familiar with the perverse nature of some societies off the island. But you are now a part of the tribe. You will live by our laws. You no longer have a husband."

"I've had enough of this!" one of the men yelled, standing up and stomping forward as he wiped bits of fruit from his beard. It was weird seeing facial hair like that. Our men had to keep clean shaven, every inch of them, including their heads.

"You will be quiet and sit down," my mother commanded.

"You have no authority over me. No woman does. I want to talk to the men of the tribe."

Yep. He was one of them.

My mother laughed at this. It was not a happy laugh. It froze the blood in my veins. Even that man took pause at it. "No man has the will to command a woman here."

"Look, girly," he said, "you're pretty and all, so just let me look at you. Don't speak." He turned to the tribe and said loudly, "You can rejoice that your man is now here. I'll keep you safe, but you belong to me now. I don't know how you survived so long without a man to lead you, but I'll fill all of your needs."

With what I know now, I'm sure he thought this was a dream come true. A fantasy of his, to have an island of woman for his enjoyment. It surprises me how common that fetish is. I wonder if he realized how much he sounded like a walking and talking stereotype.

He turned to the soldier woman that was walking up to him. She was taller and more muscular than he was, but still he did not seem concerned. He actually smiled. He was excited.

"Don't you step up to me. I'm not afraid to hit a woman, you stupid cunt."

He did not see it, because I think he would have made a different decision if he did. Maybe he would have held his tongue. Our soldiers were few, partly because we did not really need soldiers for the most part, but also because their requirements to join those ranks were rare. Their body magic allowed them to alter their forms, kind of like what Emere did with her webbed fingers, but theirs was blunter. Her fist grew stone over the flesh, as solid and hard as quartz.

She swung at him, and he seemed honestly surprised that she did. Her fist contacted his jaw. The sound still turns my stomach just thinking of it. It was a wet sound first, like a stick hitting a piece of meat. The second sound was similar to a dried stick breaking. His jaw was dislocated and broken at once. It hung limply on his face, and he screamed as he fell to his hands and knees.

The screaming did not last long as another of the soldiers came up and drove a spear through his back and out the front of his chest. It was struck with such force that it passed through his body all the way into the ground. His body went limp and hung on the shaft. She left it there, leaving him stuck like a boar.

"Now," my mother said, continuing like there was no interruption.

The survivors all stared at the dead man, eyes wide in disbelief, hands covering mouths left agape. Eyes showed shock, horror, and despair.

"The men will live their lives out with our men. You will be servants of the tribe. This means you will be at the beck and call of any woman of age for whatever her desire is. For cleaning her hut, washing her clothes, bringing her food, breeding when allowed by the Blessed. This will be your lives for now until then end. There is no escape of this. Most men quickly accept this to be their fate, as the Sun made all men the servants of woman."

"Madam," the mother of the girl I saved said.

"You may speak," my mother replied.

"My name is Gloria. This is my daughter Gina."

"For now," my mother said. "Until we give you new names."

"And he is Dustin." She pointed to one of the men. "He is my husband. Surely he will be allowed to live with us. We're a family."

"He is not called Dustin anymore. Men do not have names here. And you will not get any sympathy calling a man part of your family. Men live to serve only. They are not people like you and me." My mother scowled in disdain. "Family is your new sisters, not any man."

"Haven't we all felt that way at one point about men?" Gloria asked. "But we don't throw them away. We hold them close and love them for their stupidity. Please don't do this."

"Men are little more than domesticated animals."

"No!" Gloria yelled. "He is my husband."

"And again you say that word," my mother said. "What does it mean?"

"I love him, and he loves me. We have dedicated out lives to each other."

My mother laughed then. It was not a joyous thing, but a thing of disdain, of disbelief. It was the kind of laugh someone does when presented with an impossibility spoken as an absolute truth. "Surely you are joking."

"No. He is mine, and you will not take him away from me!"

"I am giving you this one chance to leave it be."

Grasping her mother's arm with both hands, holding her close and in front of her like a shield, Gina pleaded, "Mom. Don't do this now. We need to live. We can figure this out, but only if we survive."

"Wise words," mother said. "You should listen to your child."

Gloria screamed, "I will not give Dustin up!"

"Just remember that was your decision."

The soldiers pushed Gina away from her mother and grabbed Gloria, one holding on to each arm.

"I strip you of your right to Rite of Passage. You will not be given a name. You will not become a sister. You will be punished in accord to our laws. The man in question shall carry the same punishment for consorting to be more than the animal he is."

Gloria stood tall with her chin up in defiance. "And what is this punishment?"

"You will be tied to the beach during low tide and left."

The color drained from Gloria's face at that, but Gina looked back and forth between her mother and mine. "What does that mean?"

Gloria looked at her daughter. "You will survive this,

33

darling. Be strong. You can take anything thrown at you and make it good."

The girl stomped toward the Blessed. "What does that mean?" she demanded, shrieking at them.

Mother regarded her with a soft expression. "They are to be executed, given to the sea and Sun for their crimes."

Gina stood apart from everyone else, looking dejected and tossed away. She demanded, "What crimes?"

"Men are animals," mother replied. "One does not consort with an animal in anything but work. We understand the perverse nature of the outside world and forgive those sins to all new sisters taking the Rite, but those deviant natures must be left."

"You can't do this!"

Her mother said, "It's okay, darling. Be strong. We survive if you survive."

"No, Mom!" she yelled. "Dad, talk some sense into her."

"Be strong like your mother says," Dustin said; though he sounded resigned to his fate, his face betrayed his terror.

"If you want to see them forgiven, a sister of the tribe can demand clemency," mother said.

"Then I demand clemency," Gina said.

"You are not a sister."

"What do I have to do?"

34

Mother replied, "You pass the Rite. It does not have to be done now. You will remain a child to the tribe until it is done, but children cannot do this thing you wish."

"I'm not afraid! What must I do?"

"You will wait until you bleed. If needed, their punishment will be held until then," mother said.

Gina's cheeks turned red, and she looked away. "Probably in a couple days."

"When it begins, you will be given the Chief of Ghosts to eat. That will pull back the physical veil of the world and show you reality."

"You're going to drug me?"

"Don't do this," her father said.

"Dad, I can't just not try," Gina said, though her voice sounded shaky.

Mother continued, "You will be stripped naked and taken to the far side of the lagoon and left. You need to swim back to the beach."

"Naked, menstruating, drugged, and swimming in the ocean?" Gina asked, tears starting to run down her face. "Are there sharks there?"

"There shouldn't be. Not in the lagoon," mother answered. "When you reach the shore, you will be cut, a horizontal slice above your labia. It marks you a woman of the tribe. Only then can you demand anything of the Blessed."

Gina hung her head, and she sobbed. "I can't do that."

"That is your choice. Live with the consequences of it." Commanding to the soldiers, mother said, "Take them away."

"Wait!" Gina shouted. "Isn't there anything else I can do?"

"No," my mother said. "The only other option is for one of the sisters to speak up on your behalf."

Gina looked the tribe women over. "Please," she pleaded. "Please speak for my parents. They are good people. They are all I have."

Mother said, "We are good people as well. And they are not all that you have anymore. You have us now."

"Will anybody speak up for my family?"

I know, most would think I surely said something, but I didn't. Please remember, my whole life was Tribe over Pride. This was my family. What she asked was offensive, that she would accept a man over the tribe, even to someone like me who was a relative loaner. The tribe was still my family.

Nobody spoke on her behalf, so the soldiers holding on to Gloria began to walk off with her. Two others pulled Dustin to his feet and followed them.

"Please don't!" Gina fell to her knees and pleaded.

Mother ignored her and continued on. "Is there anyone who wishes to intercede?"

Three women stepped forward from the crowd. "We would like to argue for a different fate for one of these men."

Gina cried in relief. "Thank you!"

Mother asked, "Which one?"

"Him." The girl pointed to one of the men who was sitting near the food spread.

"No!" Gina screamed. "Save my parents!"

They continued on like she had not spoken at all. "He has brought us something new."

"What is it?"

"This," one of the girls walked forward, holding out something.

Mother took it from her and turned it in her hands, examining it. It was two pieces of bread, sliced thin, with meats, cheeses, and fruits pilled on it. Mother lifted it to her mouth and took a bite. Her eyes widened. "This is good."

"He calls it a sandwich," one of the three girls said.

"What is your request?"

"Make him a cook. He can make these sandwiches for the tribe. It benefits us all."

"This is abnormal, but I will allow it presuming he

maintains proper deference to the women of the tribe and never forgets he is still just a man."

He stood and said, "Thank you," to Mother.

"You will not be given the Rite of Passage, so you will not have a say in the tribe's business. You will remain a child but will be given leave of a man's role as long as you please us with your works. In this case, you should be given a name. What would fit one such as you? A man, but one respected. Ah," she exclaimed. "We shall call you Tane. Your old name will be forgotten as you will be Tane to all."

"Mother," one of my sisters called out. It was Emere, to my displeasure. "May I be tasked in showing him around so he knows where everything is and how he is supposed to behave? Even giving the privilege of a child, he should understand the expectations of his position."

Mother nodded. "So be it. Daughter Emere, show him the island and teach him our ways."

Chapter 4

I was down at the beach well after sunset. Most of my sisters had already left the community fires and retired to their huts for the evening. I waited until late so nobody would be around to see me. I needed to keep my actions hidden.

It was not pitch black as the moon was out and the clouds were gone, making the sands and water glow. There were glowing coals from the fires still, but no open flames anymore other than those on the ship itself. That would burn for at least another day, but it should sink soon either way.

It was easy to see the beach under all that light, though it wasn't as bright as last night had been with the flames. It was more evenly lit now under moonlight, and without the shadowed areas between the bright lights, it was much easier to see. Of course, the lack of downpour also helped. Needless to say, everything looked different than it did the prior night. That would prove to be the biggest problem in finding what I was looking for.

As planned, nobody else was about the beach. Half of the tribe spent the day down there scavenging through the refuse from the ship wreck, taking anything that would be useful to share with the tribe. Everybody was dead tired by this time, and searching through the darkness of night would be inefficient. I mean, the only reason to do that would be because someone wanted to hide something. Apparently I was the only one who wished to do that.

Things had been moved around a lot. I was looking for the piece of ship I pulled that girl Gina out from underneath. It shifted from my digging, so I had a hard time locating it. I was looking for the smooth white hull that made up the most of it. There were a few pieces that looked like it, but only a few, and they were spread over the beach. I walked along them, stopping at each that could have been it and kicked around in the sand.

I ended up walking up and down the beach a couple times, ultimately dismissing them. I did find it, eventually. I knew it because of an indent dug out from under it. Its weight had shifted since last night with the lapping of the sea and fell into the hole.

40

Not much seemed disturbed around it save a few footprints that moved past it and continue on. Most of my sisters must have been hunting elsewhere on the beach. I got down on my hands and knees and began to dig in the sand, searching for the buried treasure I hoped was still there.

There was no way for me to mark the spot clearly. As the water comes and goes out from both the tide and waves, it would wash away any marking in the sand. Any item, like a stick, would just be as easily carried away. Or it could be obvious to one of my sisters, meaning they may figure out someone was trying to come back for this. That would be bad.

My thoughts drifted as I dug. I had been with Lelei for a few months now. I don't normally stay with a girlfriend for so long. In fact, I've been with her for longer than I ever have with anyone before. There was just something about her. She was so fun and kind. She was also a terrific lover. She truly made me happy. But so had many of the others. I felt like maybe I was allowing this to go on too long. I was too comfortable around her.

If I got too comfortable with someone, I was much more likely to mess up, and my secret would be discovered. I've kept it secret for a decade. The whole tribe would call for my blood if it ever was found out. Even Lelei would want me dead. I worried about what would happen to her if she found out and did not turn

41

me in. That would be a terrible burden to lay on her. Perhaps it was time to move on.

I really did like her though. It just was not safe for either of us. I knew what I had to do, but that didn't mean it was easy. Tomorrow. I would do it tomorrow. She was fine before having me in her life and she would be fine afterward.

When I found my treasure, my mind snapped back to the task at hand. I pulled the item I had hidden last night out of the sand. It was wet, but such things were waterproof. We don't have electronics on the island other than what we found in wrecks, and most of it would be ruined by water. A few items would survive it, and these always do, to the tribe's discontent.

It was a two-way radio. With it, I could talk to ships and airplanes traveling near the island. That was why it was a taboo, though this one would not get me killed. Probably. As long as I didn't actually contact anyone with it. They wouldn't let me keep it though, that's for sure.

Our island was thought deserted with nothing of value on it. We have kept it this way by not letting anyone leave once they were here. It was our separation from the rest of the world that kept us safely tucked away. A radio like this could end it all for us.

I wasn't planning on using the radio, mind you. I just wanted it. It represented a freedom, a scary freedom, but freedom nonetheless. It comforted me knowing I had a way to run if my big secret was ever discovered. I probably wouldn't do me any good. But I felt better having it.

I put it in my leather satchel and headed off the beach. I stepped foot in the forest and began the walk back to the village to hide the radio in my hut.

On the east side of the island was the lagoon. It was a bay that dipped into land, leaving points jutting into the ocean that were closed by coral, separating the lagoon from the rest of the ocean. It was the one place to swim without having to worry about sharks or jellyfish. We didn't have problems with them usually, but it was nice to have a safe place.

I was passing by the lagoon when a sound caught my attention. It was human, but it sounded weird.

I crept that way, moving silently like when I was hunting. With the amount and volume of noise I was hearing, I didn't think whoever was there would have heard me anyway, but I wanted to be careful. It sounded like someone was being attacked, which would mean I would need to help.

I crawled into bushes at the edge of the trees and peered out, looking over the beach. There were two people there. I squinted my eyes, straining to see in the darkness. I knew them. It was Emere and that man from the ship. The one who made the food.

He was on top of her, and she was shouting at him. No, this wasn't sex. He was attacking her! Why would she bring him down here? He was new. He wasn't broken in yet. Such men were wild and dangerous.

I had to help her.

She got the upper hand then, rolling him on to his back and straddling him, holding him down. She put her hands on his chest to hold him in place. I expected her to punch him then...but she didn't. She just slid her hips up and down, grinding against his pelvis. She cried out then, and that was not the sound of struggle, but ecstasy.

She was naked, I now saw, as was he. They were fucking. His dick was inside her! I know that sounds obvious, but at the time it wasn't to me. Men were service animals for us. They cleaned. They moved things. The only time they had sex with a woman was when she wanted a child. I mean, there were deviants that would rather have sex with a man, but they were ostracized by the tribe if they acted out those fantasies. Men were not for pleasure. But I had a vision of the opposite being true glazed into my eyes. I had never seen such a thing before. That's why it didn't immediately become obvious to me what was happening. Civilized women don't do what she was doing.

44

I never considered a man touching me like that. I was confused watching it, his penis stiff and...and large, inside her. At least I thought it was large. I could only see the base of it as it pulled out and pushed back in her. It looked wide. How could that fit? I thought it had to hurt, being stretched like that, but nevertheless I felt a twinge, an itch between my own legs from watching. I flushed, thinking my body was reacting like that to a man in the throes of pleasure. That couldn't be right. But it was. It seemed so wrong, but I liked it.

I suppose that shouldn't have surprised me. I had never once thought about a man as a possible sexual partner before. Most of our men were docile, domesticated animals, not sexual people, but I was seeing proof that they could be.

She rocked on him, her hands extended forward to his chest, holding herself up. Her pelvis thrust back and forth as she humped him, thrusting it in and out. Her lips were parted, and she moaned. No, this was more than moaning. She was nearly screaming in ecstasy. She was in pleasure throes I had never experienced before. I briefly wondered if she was faking it, but why would she? And if she was, she was really good.

What could that feel like, such a large fleshy member pushing into my neither regions? I felt the twinge again at that. Obviously my body wanted to know. I was kind of disgusted from

45

the whole thing, especially when she leant down and kissed him. Kissed him! It was so despicable. How could she degrade herself like this?

And yet...

I couldn't help myself. I couldn't look away. I took my top off, bearing my breasts to the night air. I grabbed one of my nipples and pinched lightly, making it pucker. That made it worse. I don't know why I didn't expect that. I pulled up my skirt as I crouched down. My feet were planted on the ground, and my knees spread to allow my fingers to caress into my cleft. I was so wet! My fingers fiddled my hood, making my clit swell.

I breathed deeply, smelling the sweetness of my own sex as I rubbed it and watched them bump against each other and shout and moan. My body reacted in excitement watching his stiff member inside her. I no longer thought about how wrong it was. I could only think about how much I wanted it for myself.

I found myself feeling jealous of Emere. She was with this man, feeling the pleasure I desired. I vowed then to take him away from her. I would claim him as mine and feel his strong hands on my breasts as I watched him do to her. I would feel his throbbing shaft inside me. I would swell around him, try to push him out while he forced himself back in. I wanted this more than anything else I have ever desired before. I was disgusted and elated all the same.

My fingers pinched harder on my nipples, and my rubbing hand moved furiously with my need. The pleasure swelled up in me like a wave, lapping on my senses, receding and building back up in grate rolls. And then the pleasure exploded in my body, and my furiously moving hand stilled, the muscles no longer responding to my need anymore.

A gasp escaped my lips as I lowered myself to the ground. My butt planted in the wet dirt, and my legs remained wide open as my stilled hand was able to keep the pressure, not allowing the orgasm to recede for many long seconds.

When my peak finally waned away, my eyes went wide, and my hand covered my mouth when I realized how loud I just was. I looked out from the bushes and saw both of their heads turned my way, looking for who made that sound. I grabbed my stuff and ran on weak legs.

I was far away before I stopped, collapsing to the mossy ground and just giggled at the absurdity of it all. Emere was with that man, a man the Blessed would not have approved. She broke a taboo, and I wanted to steal it from her for my own. Absurd, but no less true.

I smiled again, wondering if my orgasm had stolen Emere's. That thought made me even happier as I put my clothes back on to return home. I didn't want to show up naked. Lelei was likely to ask questions, and I did not want to explain this. I walked home, still feeling tingly from my release. I just hoped my legs would be back to normal in the morning.

Chapter 5

The next morning, I woke up next to Lelei. She was asleep when I left last night and still sleeping when I got back. If she did wake up while I was gone, it would be easy enough to tell her I went to the latrine. I just had to pee.

I lay there, looking at her. She was so beautiful, not in the way some women can make your heart ache just by looking at their face, but in that innocent, nice girl look. She smiled so sweetly and was always so concerned about others. It was a shame, knowing I would one day hurt her. I knew I should end it before the problems began, because the more time we would be together the worse the pain would be. I just didn't want to leave her. I was being selfish, keeping this relationship going. She could have been the one.

I did wonder to myself if that could have been the truth of the matter though. If that was the case, would I want to take the sandwich man from Emere for my own? Wouldn't loving someone make me not want another? I was such a child then.

Either way, I understood that breaking up was not about Lelei at all. It was all about me and what I wanted. It was selfish of me. I couldn't keep my secret from her forever if we remained together. She would stumble upon it at some point. Even if she decided to stay with me after she knew, she would be in danger then as well.

Her eyes opened and looked at me. I could feel her breath on my face. She smiled. I leaned in and kissed her.

"I want to do something special today," I said.

"Really?" She sounded very excited. "Does that mean I get to put a finger in your ass today?"

She was being serious. I did not understand that. She brought it up once a week at least. I couldn't say it was not my thing. I've never had my butt penetrated before, so I didn't know if I would enjoy it or not, but it did not sound fun. Sure, she did play with it sometimes, rubbing along the outside, but putting a finger inside it? That just sounded uncomfortable.

I blinked a few times before replying, "Not what I had in

mind."

"Oh. But still..."

I ignored that, though my butt clenched at the thought. Maybe, some day. Not today though. "I was thinking we should go see the new guy."

"The guy that makes the...sandwiches?"

"Yeah! That's what they were called," I replied.

"Oh." She paused. "Okay. Yeah, let's go. They called him Tane, I think." She sounded a little disappointed, but at least she also sounded genuine about wanting to try a sandwich.

We got dressed, which involved a bunch of harmless pinching and butt slapping, and maybe even a licked nipple. She wasn't expecting that. It made her jump. It was awesome.

We left the hut and headed toward the center of the tribe. The utility buildings there were larger than the personal huts as these were for community use. Weavers, thatches, cooks. They all worked out of the buildings here, so each building was made to accommodate one craft or another. The cookeries had fireplaces and fire ovens with chimneys. They cooked the animals hunters like me brought back. They baked breads. They roasted bananas and peppers. Food was cooked for the full tribe, given freely to anyone who was hungry.

We found him in one of the smaller cookeries, alone. None

of the women cooks were there. That was probably telling. He may have gotten a special exemption, but that did not mean he would ever be treated to his actual station. He would always be a child to the tribe, which was far better than the other men, but he would not be treated much better than the others. In fact, he would probably be treated much worse. Men were in the cookeries helping all the time, from fetching water to cutting ingredients. He would not be given the same accommodation as them. He was their equal, but he would never be their equal.

Still, there would be some of us who would be kind to him. People like me. I was his saint. He just didn't know it yet.

He was busy kneading dough when we walked in. He was mumbling to himself and looked like he was concentrating intently on what he was doing.

"Good morning!" I said to him. I tried to not stare, because I felt like a jungle cat hunting pray.

He turned and looked at me, smiled briefly, and went back to his dough. He stared at it, not moving. His shoulders were slumped forward with his hands grabbing the table's edge. I noticed the dough looked kind of lumpy as it sat between his hands. It didn't look right.

He turned back to us. "The bread's not ready yet. And a sandwich just isn't a sandwich without bread. Can you come back a little later?"

"You didn't get in early to start making the bread?" Lelei asked.

"Nobody showed me where to work. I had to ask a lot of people, and someone eventually led me here."

"It's weird nobody else is here," Lelei said.

"There was," he grumbled.

"Where'd they go?" she asked.

"I don't know. They just left when I got here." He crossed his arms across his chest.

"Why would..." Lelei was saying.

I interrupted her before she could push that matter forward. "Well, I want to try a sandwich. Do you need any help?" I walked up next to him and placed a hand on his arm.

He uncurled his arms and seemed to relax.

"Help? Na." He shrugged my hand off. "Bread makes the sandwich. I'm just trying to get used to the flour you use here. It doesn't...rise like it does back home."

Lelei asked, "Who did you get the legacy dough from?"

"What do you mean?" he asked.

Lelei looked at me for a second before responding. "Legacy dough. You mix your dough with leftover bits from earlier dough. That's what makes the new dough rise. That, or you can start your own, but it's hard to get the right mixture of fermented fruits to get it working."

"Oh. We don't do it that way back home. My mom taught me to just put yeast in it."

Lelei asked, "What's yeast?"

"It's a powder that makes the bread rise."

"I don't know about any of that," my girlfriend said.

"I see." He turned back to his lumpy dough. "I don't think anybody is going to give me some of their dough."

"Yours isn't ready yet anyway," Lelei said. "It's all lumpy."

"Yeah," was all he said.

She cocked her head sideways and stared for an awkward moment. "Do you know how to make bread?"

He looked back to us with the saddest eyes I have ever seen on someone. He opened his mouth to answer, but nothing came out. He sighed and closed his mouth again.

"What's your name?" Lelei asked him.

"Johnny."

She shook her head. "Didn't they call you Tane?"

"Yeah."

"Have you ever made bread before, Tane?"

He shook his head. "I saw my mom do it before, but that was when I was little. I don't know how to. I'm trying my best."

"Really?" I asked him, genuinely surprised.

He snapped at me then. "I didn't know I would have to make everything from scratch!"

"Hey now!" I shot back, surprised he would take that tone with me. "You might have a special exemption, but that doesn't excuse you talking to a confirmed woman like that."

"I'm sorry." He looked almost afraid as he apologized. "Where I come from, if you needed bread, you get it at the store. There are shelves full of bread."

"We have something like that too," Lelei said. "Some women bake bread, and anyone can get what they need."

"Can I get bread from them?"

"No," Lelei said. "You work in the cookery."

I explained, "If you got bread from one of the bakers, they would have less bread for the tribe. You are expected to make sandwiches, so you need to make the sandwiches. If you took bread from a baker, we would have less prepared food, not more."

He looked back at his dough. "It is really lumpy. And it's not rising at all." He turned back to us. "Is it asking too much to see if you'll help me? I don't want to be a bother, but I don't know the rules here. I don't want to be placed with the other men. I've seen them. I don't want that."

Lelei smiled warmly. "Of course. It's kind of weird, you being given such special privilege. I want to see where this goes. So I'll get some legacy bread for you and help you make your own dough."

"I want to help too," I said. "What kind of meat are you going to use?"

"Whatever is available," he answered uncertainly.

I said, "Let me help with that. I'll catch you a boar. We'll roast it. It'll be so juicy." I emphasized the juicy bit and winked at him. He did not seem to notice. I'm sure he was distracted, but I was just starting. He wouldn't be able to ignore me for long.

Lelei left to get the legacy dough, and I walked out after her. I made sure to walk past him and pinch his butt on the way past. I swear it was made of all muscle. There wasn't a pinch of fat on that ass at all!

I walked through the village and headed out into the forest. I went west and up the slop to the mountain. That was the prime hunting area for me. Nobody else went there. It was dangerous, but I was safe. The other girls did not go there. That left a lot of game for me to take down.

I began jogging as my stride widened. My swift feet carried me deep into the forest, away from prying eyes. I smiled as I relaxed the control in my mind. I felt something snap, like a twig.

I'm sure it looks painful, my body changing like it does, but it is orgasmic. Imagine you are a wild cat, but have been lock up in a cage with a concrete floor. And then one day you get free to run on the grass. That's what it's like.

My senses sharpened. I could see farther and react faster like that. I could hear the little sounds of the forest much more. And the smells! It was so wonderful, the bouquet of aromas. There were smells I didn't even know existed before my first time changing.

I could see the glossy black hair with dark circles sprout along my arms. My fingers shortened to nubs while my fingernails grew longer and narrowed into claws, and hard pads formed on my finger tips and in my palms. I bent forward, extending my newly formed paws on the mossy forest floor and spread my gait out and ran. The air blew into me, keeping my lungs full of fresh air and pushing through the fur over my body.

I snarled in excitement, not being able to talk or shout in this form. This was my secret. This was my real taboo. I was a changeling. Some girls could grow webbing, or form rock into their flesh, or breathe under water, but I could actually become a forest cat. Nobody else could do that. And that was dangerous. As dangerous as I was like this, the tribe would be my undoing if they discovered me. This is what I hid desperately. Not even Lelei could know.

I sprinted deeper and deeper into the forest my sisters did not enter. It was a dangerous place for most of them. There were boa snakes here that had been known to take children that wandered too deeply. There were the boars themselves, with their large tusks and knife sharp cloven hooves. They would charge and gouge even a seasoned hunter if she was not careful. There were monkeys, and though they would not attack a human, they would throw down coconuts at high speeds that could cause a lot of damage. But it was the panthers, the black jaguars, my animal form, that really were the danger.

There were not many, but they did exist. They stayed mostly away from us, which was why they had become more legend than real in the tribe's eyes. I knew the truth though. There were a few. They hunted the boars and deer. They hunted other small mammals too. They hunted the monkeys. And they hunted the humans. They were the top of the food chain.

And I was accepted among them. I was seen as another forest cat. They were wary of me, just as they were wary of any of the others. The forest cats were mostly solitary and territorial, keeping to their own area around the base of the mountain, only venturing near another to mate.

I passed through the territories of the other forest cats.

They usually let me be. I did not have a territory of my own as I couldn't live like this. They seemed mostly willing to ignore me. When one appeared, I was submissive and left after they sniffed at me and growled a little, but they never did harm me. I have seen two of them fight before. I did not want to be a part of that. Their fighting was just as savage as their fucking.

I found that out the hard way. I caught the attention of one of them once, and acting submissive only seemed to excite it more. It lunged for me, and I ran. It chased me. And it kept chasing me. That was new. It hunted me all over the mountain until I was too tired to continue on. It caught me then. It tried to mount me, but I fought back. We both were tired by that time. I learned a lot that night.

I caught the scent I was looking for as I was winding up the mountain's base. It smelled musky. Male and virile. And it was angry. So hot in its temperament. I purred in anticipation as I stalked through the woods. I stayed low as I crept forward, my sharp eyes scanning the woods ahead, but it was my nose I was following. I could hear it ahead, rooting through the dirt, snorting in that way only pigs could.

I saw it then. It was covered in a thick, coarse, brown fur. Its left ear was shredded, probably from another boar fighting for a mate. Its tusks were as long as my human forearms. It was facing away from me, pushing its shovel shaped snout in the dirt, looking for roots and earthworms. Its tail stood straight up with a tuft of hair on the end, so proud, so sure of itself.

I crept closer, leaving nothing between it and me. My muscles tensed, corded up like tightly pulled rope. And I pounced. My claws tore up clods of the ground when I leapt. I dug my knife like claws into the back of the beast. It screamed in fright and pain. It tried to run, but my body weight took it down to the ground, and my teeth cut through the thick skin on the back of its head. They went deep, and the warmth of blood poured into my mouth. I felt a crunch as I crushed the poor creature's skull in my vice like mouth. It kicked feebly but little else.

I began to drag it back to the village. When I was only a little ways out, I changed back and dragged it the rest of the way. Tane was going to be so excited.

Chapter 6

The fire bathed the cookery with warbling light in that late hour. The boar roasted above it, dripping sizzling juices into the fire. The smell was amazing. So sweet and savory. I wanted to tear into it with my teeth, ripping chunks of flesh off like a wild cat. It still had to cook for hours because much of it was still undercooked, but a panther would relish such succor. Sometimes, resisting such temptation was difficult. I felt more forest cat than human somedays.

Lelei, Tane, and I sat around the fire, otherwise alone. The hut was sealed up, closing the shutters to give us privacy in our work. The other two had made bread together as I got the boar cooking. Lelei taught him how we did it on the island, and their efforts were currently in the oven, baking over glowing red coals. The work was pretty much done.

"I can't thank you two enough," Tane said.

"It's what we do," Lelei replied. She looked so relaxed. Her eyes were half-lidded, and she had a satisfied little smile on her face. It was all for doing good works.

Tane was decidedly less relaxed. "I don't think you understand." The tension in his voice was thick, and it pried Lelei's eyes open. "I wouldn't have been able to do this without your help."

"I'm sure you could," she said, trying to reassure him.

"No. I wouldn't have been able to. I don't know anything about making bread. I don't know anything about hunting. I don't know anything about cooking. I just know how to make good sandwiches. I'm sure anyone on that boat could. I don't understand how nobody has made one before me." His voice reflected growing panic.

Lelei sat forward, and her smile disappeared. "Did everyone take care of you back home or something?"

"No," Tane said. "If I needed bread, I'd just go to the store and buy some. We didn't have to make anything. You just needed to work to earn money. And if you didn't, nobody would help you."

"Come on," I said. "Nobody would help? How could you not help someone in your tribe? You see them every day! You can't just ignore their suffering."

"See them every day?" Tane asked. "I don't think you know anything about where I come from. It's not a tribe. It's a city called Arvada. It's part of Denver."

"Never heard of it," I said.

"I figured as much. Look, you can walk across this whole island in, what, half a day?"

I snorted. "If you're slow!"

"It would take you a few days to walk across Denver and the suburbs."

"What?" Lelei asked, not understanding.

"The city is many times larger than this whole island. And there is so many people there. Walk across it and you will probably not see a single person you actually know."

Lelei laughed. "Stop playing with us!"

"I'm serious." And he did look serious. He looked so intense, and I wanted him so much more for it. "It's easy to ignore people suffering when they are just faceless people you don't know and will probably never see again. In my world, if you fall down, you are mostly responsible to pick yourself up."

"Nobody will help?" Lelei asked. "Really? Nobody?"

"The government used to have programs that would help people if they fell on hard times, but they were taken away. It was too expensive."

Lelei and I looked at each other. We didn't understand terms like money and expensive. They were not a factor of life on the island. What he was talking about was so foreign to us that we could hardly even imagine what he was telling us.

"It sounds horrible!" my girlfriend said.

"It wasn't so bad. You had freedom to do pretty much whatever you wanted. You were just on your own."

"I can't imagine that," I said to him. "In the tribe, we need each other. We work together to survive. If one of us is not doing well, then we all are not doing well. How can one person have everything they could want and be happy when another has nothing?"

"Yeah. I understand. You can't say that back home though. People get labels. Not physically labeled, but if you are known as the wrong thing, life is much more difficult."

"I think I get it!" Lelei suddenly said. "That's what it's like for the men. It sounds pretty good. All that freedom. Our men don't have that."

Tane shook his head. "No. Men pretty much rule our society."

"Now you're talking fantasy!" I said, laughing it out.

"No. It's true."

"How could that be?" Lelei demanded. "Women bring life into the world. Men can't do that."

"Yeah, and women have a hard time supporting themselves when they are pregnant."

"That's a weakness in your world?" I asked, astonished.

"Yeah. They don't have much say in it either. Contraceptives are pretty much gone, and all types of abortion is illegal."

"Someone would kill their child?" Lelei's mouth was wide open in shock at the mere idea.

"They can't. Not anymore. Not legally, at least."

"But," Lelei stuttered in her frustration, "Why don't the women just use their body magic and put the men in their place. It sounds like they fucked it all up, as I would expect."

"Body magic," Tane said. "That's what you call it. You mean like when some of the women here alter their bodies."

I asked, "Like what?"

"I saw one turn her arm into rock at the trial," he said.

"Yeah? What about it?" I asked.

"I've never seen anything like that before."

"Really?" Lelei asked.

"People can't do that anywhere else," Tane said.

"That's weird. Every woman in the tribe can," Lelei said.

"Can you show me how to do it?"

I said, "Men can't do it."

He looked disappointed. "Why not?"

"Because women are the chosen people of Mother Sun," Lelei said.

Tane laughed for a second and looked back and forth between us. "You're serious."

I asked, "You don't believe in Mother Sun?"

"No."

"There's nobody here who doesn't believe in Mother Sun," Lelei said. "I don't understand how you couldn't. She's right up there I the sky."

"That's just the sun," Tane said. "It's a furnace of fiery gas."

I said. "You're just one mistake away from being with the other men. You might want to rethink what you're saying. Our sisters might not be as understanding as we are."

His face turned ashen. "I realize that. Can you tell me how you do it?"

"Do it?" I asked, waggling my eyebrows.

"Huh? Changing your bodies. How do you do it?"

Lelei said, "It's just something we...do."

"Nobody teaches you?"

I shook my head. "You breathe. Did someone teach you how to do that? It's just something our bodies do."

"Well, what kind of things can you do?"

Lelei laughed. "Asoese can't do much."

"Hey!"

"Sorry!" She pushed me playfully. "Some of us can make our bodies into rocks like you saw. Others grow claws that help with digging and climbing. Some make webbing between their fingers and toes for swimming. Others can actually breathe underwater by making gills. Some are more extreme than that, while others merely run fast or jump high."

"What do you two do?"

I said, "I react quickly. I'm more agile than anybody or anything on the island. It's why I'm a hunter. Lelei." I smiled at her and kissed her hand. "She can grow feathers. Not really useful for most things, though they can look impressive. But we've found some uses for them."

My girlfriend giggled at that.

"Can anyone turn into an animal?" Tane asked.

And that was the question. It made both Lelei and I quiet as we thought about the tribe's legends. Lelei said slowly to him, "To even talk about that is forbidden."

Tane cocked an eyebrow. "If nobody talks about it, how do you know about it?"

Lelei answered, "The elder women hold the tribe's memories as stories. They pass them down to the younger women, who must learn them to pass them on to the next generations so we don't forget who we are. They tell us the story. But we're not really supposed to talk about it."

Tane made a show of looking around the hut. "I don't see anyone around. Who'd know?"

Lelei shook her head, but I liked his thinking. "Our leaders are called the Blessed. That is any woman Mother Sun has 'blessed' with a child. When they give birth, they are no longer Blessed."

Lelei said, "When one of us is pregnant, we are closer to the Sun as anyone can be. We are creating life after all, just as She had for us."

"It was not always that way," I said. "The first women and men came to the island during a storm. They got stranded here like you and the others did. Body magic began to show up in the women shortly after. The youngest woman showed the greatest power. A number of them began changing into animals. Jaguars, bears, elk. They ended up fighting each other as children sometimes do. But in their animal forms, it became bloody. Soon,

68

only the jaguars survived, and they used their powers to make all of the others serve them. So it was, the jaguars ruled the tribe and set our original laws."

"They ruled through the power of the claw and tooth," Lelei said. "Anyone who spoke against them was killed. It was a dark time, and it lasted for a few generations. Eventually the body magic spread more evenly through the families. The jaguar family stopped being able to transform. It was merely their savagery and power that kept them in control. Most of the jaguar family was killed when the tribe revolted against them. It was unfortunate they all mostly were killed. But repressed people want revenge."

I said, "So now we are led by the Blessed. This way, any woman can help lead the tribe, and nobody stays in power forever."

Tane asked, "So nobody can transform into an animal anymore?"

"That's not entirely true," I said. That had gone on long enough. I had a mission, and it was time to get to it. I got up on my hands and knees and crawled toward Lelei, growling. "Some of us can be quite the animals when we want." Tane was between us, so I crawled into his lap. He leaned back uncertain.

I stretched and kissed Lelei, and she kissed me back. I made sure my ass was up in the air, and I waved it side to side as I kept growling. My undulations brought my rear near him, waggling in his face. He didn't touch me, but I didn't expect him to...yet.

I crawled forward more, gently pushing my girlfriend down. I straddled one of her legs, resting my knee between her legs and pushing my thigh softly against her wetness. She moaned once as I licked the bare flesh of her neck and nipped on her earlobe.

My fingers went searching. They did not immediately go to her most tender of bits. No. Oh no. I needed to play this up right. This was going to be a long night. A long and sexy night. He was scared of the tribe; that much was certain. I would need to overcome his fright, to slowly bring his loins to a boil. That way when he finally overflowed, he would make our cup runneth over as well!

My fingers traced her jaw line, running the smooth skin from below her ear, along her neck and to her chin. My lips followed, and just as often they parted for my tongue to dance along.

Lelei was not having this slow moving stuff though. She began to raise her ass off the ground, thrusting her hips skyward, rubbing her welcoming bud against my thigh. She wanted it badly. But she was going to play this my way tonight. She would have to wait.

I moved my leg from between hers and sat straddle across her belly. She reached up and under my wrap and let my breasts fall out. Her hands ran along them. Her fingers stretched to the sides, moving up along my chest and cupping me. Her thumb and middle finger on both hands rubbed my nipples, sending tingles along the tips of my chest and down my shins. I moaned, despite my best efforts to not.

This was not going right! She was not playing fair! She never really did.

I grabbed her soft mounds, much less playful than she was with mine, and I pinched hard. Her mouth opened wide in a gasp as her head went back. She moaned again. Why couldn't she play a little harder to get?

I screamed then.

I wasn't paying enough attention. I was not expecting it when one of her hands reached up my skirt to flick my clit. She apparently thought I wanted it rough. No. No. No. She was going to be punished for ruining my game.

I grabbed Lelei's arms and held them down above her head. Scooting forward, walking on my knees, I pinned her hands down under my legs and placed my musky sex over her face. I smiled at her like the little devil I was. Her eyes went wide in surprise, but I suppose it was the good type of surprise. I lowered myself onto her face, my labia spreading as the heat ran through me. I rubbed my lips against hers.

Her tongue flickered out, and I fell forward to my hands to hold myself up. On my hands and knees with Lelei's face locked between my legs, her tongue worked over my pink pearl. I realized I had lost control of the situation. How was this going to work? I needed to slowly work this up, teasing him as best I could. What about this would turn him on?

Apparently something did.

Lelei gasped. I looked down at her face, half hidden in my tender folds. I was confused at first until I felt the hand grab my ass. I looked behind me. Tane was holding my ass in one hand, and his face was buried in my girlfriend's pussy. I would have celebrated that it worked, but he was touching the wrong one of us.

Lelei started to struggle. She probably realized what was happening, and she didn't seem to share the same fantasy. Men in general disgusted her sexually. But I could work with this. I didn't let her up. I held her down and kept rubbing my heat over her face. She struggled a little, but Tane was holding her bottom half down as well as he lapped at her like a thirsty dog.

Despite herself, she began to moan, and I mean really

moan. She couldn't move, but she tried. The most movement she could do was the twitching in her limbs, and they were twitching furiously. The carnal pleasure ran through her, and she began to shout out. The vibrations of her voice rippled through my whole body from clit and ass to nose. I was about to lose myself as well. I wasn't ready yet.

I got off her before I released. It was disappointing to stop so close to my own climax, but I wanted that only when he was inside me. No longer held down, Lelei remained laying there; she merely rolled onto her side and sighed contentedly. She smiled sleepily at me.

I looked back at Tane. He was mostly naked as he only wore his loincloth, but his stem was pushing that away, making it useless as a cover. I stepped to him, still naked and wet and needy. He looked worried, like a hunted animal who realized it's time was up. His time was, just not as he may have been worried. He stood up as I stalked him. He stepped back a few steps, uncertain of my intention. I dropped to my knees in front of him and pulled on the string holding on his bit of clothing.

It fell loose, and I placed my hand on him, grasping his erection. It was huge. I wasn't exactly sure what I should do with it, so I looked at it. It was an ugly thing really. A long shaft with veins running down it like hands that were used for hard work every day. The shiny tip had a ridge around it, and the skin was darker than the rest. Below his manhood were the two biggest balls I had ever seen before. I didn't sleep with men before now, but I had seen many of them naked. His sack hung heavily. I didn't realize it would be so wrinkly up close. I was fascinated. I ran my hand over his sack, lightly tugging on it and cupping his balls. It felt like two eggs in a cloth.

I wanted him so badly. I don't know what came over me at that moment. I had heard stories of women doing this, but I couldn't imagine why a woman would want to. I couldn't explain it then either if I had to. I just knew I wanted to. Much like many of the taboos I enjoyed, I suppose.

I opened my mouth and took his rod inside. I tasted it. It was salty, but not unpleasant. I moved up and down on it while one hand moved with my mouth along the shaft. I bobbed my head on it, pushing it into my throat. It was...weird. I kind of liked it. But it was not the physicality of the whole thing that I liked. It was him. I had him by the balls, quite literally as my other hand grabbed them. He moaned and swayed to my movement. I controlled his whole body though my mouth on his member. I felt powerful. I was in control. But I wanted more.

And so did he, apparently. He pulled out of my mouth and pushed me down. He did not go for my breasts as a woman lover would have. He did not put his face between my legs, or even his hands. He lay across me, between my legs, and his mouth found mine. I could smell and taste Lelei on him. I breathed her scent in deeply. If I didn't want him before then, that would have pushed me over the ledge.

He pushed forward on me. I rolled my hips up and wrapped my legs around his midsection. What happened next surprised me. I should have known. It's what I wanted, but it was so abrupt.

My lips parted as his thickness pushed through them. I felt it rub against my entrance. It pushed slightly, and I widened for it, hugging him. It put more pressure on me, forcing me to spread open farther, wider than I had ever been. And the pleasure I experienced was incredible. When fingers would go inside me, they would not force me apart so greatly. This pushed against every direction I had, and it pushed in deep. I was worried for a second then. It looked so long that surely it couldn't all fit inside me. But it kept pushing in, even when I thought it could not go in farther, it did. I swear I felt it in my throat it was so deep.

My moist walls pushed back, and I felt him pulling out. But that was only to thrust back inside me even farther. His hips surged like waves against the beach of my womanhood. He humped me, thrusting his throbbing manhood inside and out, stretching me with his carnal knowledge. His whole body did not move atop of me like I imagined it would. It was his hips that moved, and they pounded against me. His balls slapped against me as he thrust. Pounding me into the ground.

It welled up inside me quickly, probably because Lelei brought me to the brink already. Against my muscles trying to push it out and him thrusting in though my defenses, his penis fucked me hard, and I had no chance. I came. I came hard.

I gushed all over him as my body twitched and contorted around him. Like my vagina forming to him, my body formed around his body as well, arms and legs around his body, holding him like I was afraid to ever let him go. He kept pounding into me as the orgasm overtook everything about me, leaving nothing but the memory of pleasure behind. When I finally relaxed, he pulled out and grunted. I sat up and watched his pecker flex, bobbing up and down. And it squirted milky fluid out. It shot onto my stomach in a warm and sticky mess. As it bobbed up and down, he squirted again, and again, and each time less came. He then went limp, and I laid back. I had never felt so content in my life.

I never knew it about me, but I really loved penis.

Chapter 7

We slept there that night with him. None of us had the energy or drive to attempt anything else. The three of us were wrapped up into each other, our naked limbs entwined like tree branches. There was kissing, licking, caressing, and sucking going on all through the night, though it stayed fairly mellow. But there were at least two more orgasms. I say that with confidence as I had one, and I gave Tane one as well. His was...stickier, and very volatile. His cock tensed and swelled and bounced up, ejaculating more each time.

But morning did eventually come. The great thing about being a hunter was I worked on my own schedule dependent on the needs of the tribe. That was not the case with either Tane or

Lelei. His bread was already cooked though, and the boar was done roasting. He only needed to do preparation work at that point, cutting meat and bread, so he was not in a hurry as it would be noon before anyone came calling. Lelei was a clothes-maker though. She worked with a handful of other woman, and they all worked together to make sure the tribe did not run out of clothes.

She extracted herself from our naked pile and pulled on her clothes from yesterday. Her hair looked ruffled, but I got up as well and ran my fingers through it a few times for her. She looked presentable. Not wonderful, but presentable. Well, she always looked wonderful, even when a mess. With a kiss to me, she left the cookery.

With her gone, I began putting my clothes back on. Tane lay there, watching me. I could see the disappointment in his eyes as I got dressed. I had him last night. It was even better than I could imagine. But I already had him. Did I still want that anymore? I found that I did. Maybe this wasn't a passing thing for me. That realization was a big surprise.

I was staring at him. Actually, I was staring at his penis. I turned red, suddenly embarrassed. Why would I feel that way? It was only a few hours ago that I was touching that magnificent prick. This was awkward, and I think that was my problem more than anything else.

He sat up and rubbed the sleep from his eyes. I was about to leave in silence, but he began to talk then.

"Thank you."

I flashed him a lewd smile. "And thank you!"

"What? Oh. No. That's not what I meant, but yes, thank you for that too." He smiled back, but his was warm and not overtly sexual. "I meant to thank you and Lelei for the help. I don't know if I could have gotten this all done without your help."

I shrugged it off. "Lelei doesn't like to see others suffer."

"And you?"

I barked a short laugh. "Depends who it is."

Someone knocked on the hut by the door. Tane walked over to it and pulled the shutter open, letting the light in. Emere was there. She looked at him and smiled warmly. And then she noticed me. The smile slackened, becoming little more than a piece of absentminded jewelry she wore.

"I came to see how you are holding up," she said to him. Her eyes kept darting between us.

"I'm doing well," he said, surprisingly at ease, contrasting my tension.

"Yeah," I said. "Lelei and I were here with him last night."

Her eyes scanned the cookery quickly. Not finding evidence of any sordid behavior, they finally rested on the boar.

"Did you hunt that for him? To make sandwiches with?"

"Yeah," I replied. "Some of us swim well, whereas some others can take down a wild boar." I shrugged, showing mild disinterest.

"And some of us are just wild bores!" she spat.

Tane looked between us, just now noticing something was not right.

"What was it you needed?" I asked her.

"It was my job to make sure he was shown around, after all. I just wanted to make sure he is adjusting fine."

"Oh, he's doing just fine."

She blinked slowly while looking at me and then locked him in his gaze. "I wasn't looking for her opinion. I'm here for your benefit."

Tane said, "Well, she's right. And we have a lot of things we're working on. Was there something else you needed?"

She scowled at both of us. "I have everything I need." She stomped out of the cookery, and Tane closed to shutter.

"She didn't seem so unpleasant the other day."

"I bet she didn't," I replied insinuatingly.

"What?"

I winked at him.

"That was you in the bu... I have no idea what you are

talking about!"

"I bet," I said through laughter.

"I know I already said it, but again, thank you."

"It's no big thing."

"For me, it is. Look, this is hard for me to say. I'm usually quite confident back home. But here, I don't know what I'm doing. I'm scared. I don't know what is going to happen to me, or if I will ever get back home again."

"You won't. Nobody has ever left the island," I said. "You need to figure out how you will carve a life out here with us."

"I don't know how long I can survive here. I feel that any little thing that goes wrong will be used as proof that I should be put with the other men. I don't think I could live like them. I need to be free."

"It's not as bad as you make it."

"Haven't you ever thought what it would be like to be a man here? I can see it clearly. The men are slaves. They have no control over their lives. I can't lose my freedom. I wouldn't survive."

"Just keep making sandwiches," I suggested.

"And how long until they have some woman start making them and I get thrown aside? Oh shit! And I'm sure Emere isn't going to be easy on me either now. No. I have no say in my own life here. I just want to go home." He put his arms across his knees and rested his head on them. When he looked back up, there were tears in his eyes. "I miss my friends. I miss my apartment. I miss my fucking cat, Kirby!"

"Tell me about where you came from. And I don't mean how big it was. Tell me what your life was like."

"I haven't had a girlfriend in a while. My last was Rose, but that was months ago. We're still friends, kinda. We have many of the same friends. We knew each other for a while before we dated. I really miss my best friends though. Jimmy. I played videogame with him all the time. We were playing *GTA V*. A lazy Sunday afternoon sitting on my ragged couch in front of my TV. I went out playing pool with Jessie and Brie, and Nick came sometimes. And Matt at work was always a blast." He became lost in thought and stopped talking.

"What work did you do?"

He laughed. "I made sandwiches. Sub sandwiches. I worked at a sub shop. It didn't pay much, but it took care of the rent and allowed me to go out on the weekends. I went to a couple bars and clubs occasionally. I actually put money away for a full year to afford this fishing trip. Deep sea fishing. I don't even really like to fish. It was just a fairly cheap boat trip. I wanted to try something new." He wiped his tears away. "But now I'm here.

Everything is still there. How long will it be until everyone thinks I'm dead?"

I couldn't help but think of my own situation faced with that comment. How long until everyone thought he was dead? They would care. He had people that cared for him, that would miss him if he was dead. Maybe that would was not so bad.

That struck me for one simple fact. Who in the tribe would care if I died? Some would now, but that was only because they didn't know I was a panther. If that came out, even those I was the closest with would want me dead. My friends. My sisters. They would kill me themselves. And no one would grieve for me. No one would have kind thoughts after my violent passing. And all because of how I was born, because of something I had no choice in. How was that fair?

Fuck 'em. Fuck 'em all!

"What if I told you there is a way to contact someone off island?"

He said, "If there is, they won't let me use it."

"And what if I said it is not the tribe's?"

He leapt up and grasped my shoulders with each hand, holding firm but not hard. He pleaded, "Please. If you can, help me get home!" His voice was full of such despair. "I probably could live on this island, but not under such stress and constant terror. It will drive me mad or kill me."

I made a rash decision when I told him to get dressed.

I led him from the cookery to my hut. A few saw us make our way, but most just smiled at me and ignored him. I think I could understand where he was coming from. I never really thought about it before though. Men weren't really people to me. They were animals to make our lives better. How was I supposed to know any better? All the men I ever interacted with never really spoke to me. They weren't allowed to. They never asked anything of me. They never gave me any sign they weren't happy with how things were.

I suppose some might have, just not so obviously. Most of them probably knew what was expected of them and knew swift punishment was in store to do something otherwise. They understood well enough that if they wanted to survive, they had to stay in line and listen to the women. That was their only option.

Occasionally a man would act out. I don't know what they did to those men, but I don't think I ever saw them again. I may have though. I never really remembered what any single man looked like other than the one that cleaned my hut. It didn't ever matter. It was hard to know one from the other as they didn't have names even. What did they need them for?

It was terrible to be born with a penis. You were not a

84

person. You were a nameless animal, destined to serve at any woman's needs. Damn your ambition and desires. And we should have understood. In the past, most of the women in the tribe were treated poorly because they lacked the superb powers of the shape shifting family. It was a lack of power that impoverished those women. And we did the same to the men, because for some reason they did not have the body magic at all.

I did play with the idea, for only a moment but it did pass my thoughts, that I could us my powers to take over and liberate the men. But there was only one of me, and the tribe would overwhelm me easily. The shape shifters that used to rule the tribe were still few, but many more than just me.

Inside my hut, I unburied the radio from the sand below the grass floor. I handed it to him, and he took it like a lifeline to a drowning man. He turned a dial on the top of the radio, and an artificial sound filled the hut. He pushed a button on the side and began talking franticly.

"SOS! SOS! SOS!" he said quickly. He then looked at the radio expectantly. It made no sounds at all now. "Oh," he said as he took his finger off of the transmit button, and static filled the hut again. He tried again, calling out SOS into the radio. Static was the only reply.

Tane fiddled with the buttons on the front of the device,

changing the channel it was set to. "SOS!" he called into it again, and again he only received static back.

I sat down and watched him. He changed the channel and called out. Changed the channel and called out. Changed the channel and called out. Changed the channel and called....

I woke up to him kneeling over me, pure bliss on his face. "I did it!"

"Wha...?" I'm not the most coherent person when I wake up.

"I contacted a ship! They are coming to pick me up. I'm going to be rescued."

"That's great!" I said. "You just need to promise me you won't tell anybody about the island."

"Of course!" he replied. "I'll tell them there are cannibals or something to keep anyone from coming back. But I'm going home!"

In his excitement, he kissed me. I was surprised. I know that I was kissing him a lot last night, but I didn't expect that. That moment was gone. I put a hand on his chest and pushed him back. "No. Not now." It did not feel right. I knew Lelei and I were not going to last much longer, mostly because I couldn't allow it to. Sleeping with him, without her joining in, would be cheating.

He didn't say anything, but he pushed back against my

hand and kissed me again. It was full of a terrible passion, a great need. Struggling, I pushed him off again. "I can't do this."

Tane grabbed my hands and held them above my head. He then kissed me again, though this time is was softer. His lips moved off mine and found my earlobe. He pulled the soft flesh into his mouth and suckled it while nibbling softly. I wanted him to stop, but I also didn't. I couldn't do this to Lelei though. I fought to get my hands free. His grip was just too strong.

He moved to my neck and nibbled and sucked. Each second made my core tingle. My body moved to him, arching up. My left leg curled around his waist. I wanted him so badly. I needed to pull my clothes off and...no! Lelei...cheating...

I rolled onto my belly, finally getting my hands freed. I tried to crawl from under him. He sat back and grabbed my ass cheeks and played with them. He pulled off one hand and spanked me with it. Hard. It stung, and I loved it. He spanked me again, making it sting more. He hit the other cheek then, and I cried out. He had to let go. He had to stop. And I didn't want him to quit.

I tried to crawl away again, getting up on my knees. He grabbed my waist from behind and held my rear, giving him access to my rump. He pulled off my skirt, leaving me exposed. And he took advantage of that to my great pleasure.

His hand caressed my valley from behind. I pushed my ass

back toward him, and he slipped two fingers inside my flower. My head hung down, and my breaths came ragged. He grabbed my ass again, and I came back to my better senses. I jerked forward, pulling his fingers out of me. I lay there and tried to crawl away again. He jumped on top of me, the weight of his body holding me down. His hand tangled itself in my short hair and held my head, turning it to the side. He bit down hard on my neck and licked my cheek.

Tane pulled off me a little, lifting some of his weight. He shuffled around and then placed his mass back across my bare back. His cock was loose, and it was poking at my ass.

Oh, I wanted him bad!

He forced my legs apart slightly, and his curved manhood prodded me, pushing against my labia. It slid easily through my moist folds and entered me. It was like I was a sheath for his sword, how perfectly it fit me. Tane pushed in hard, filling me with his size. He laid across me, his head with my head, his torso down my back, and his legs along mine. He thrust, rubbing against my whole body with his scepter matching the stride inside.

I felt my pleasure building, making me swell around his member. "Oh, yes!" I moaned. I was right there. I was going to cum in perfect bliss.

And then he pulled out.

88

He fucking pulled out!

I felt it wash away, the sweetness of an orgasm. All of that work, all of that pleasure, denied. He wasn't done yet. I wouldn't allow it, but before I could do anything, he shifted his weight again. He pulled our sweaty bodies apart and crawled up me a little and lay back down. His prick, wet with my juices, slid between my butt and poked at my backside. He pushed, and I felt pressure on my opening, trying to force itself inside my ass.

I couldn't believe it. It was too big! Could that really fit in me? "No! Don't! Not there!" I panted to him, but like before, he wasn't interested in listening. I thought I had made him mine, but he had actually made me his, to do with as he pleased. And I was excited for it. Lelei would be so angry that someone claimed my ass before her, and it was bigger than her fingers I had denied.

I bit my lip against the butterflies in my stomach, and that changed into an open mouthed gasp as he pushed hard. The pressure was stunning as his head pushed my hole open. It hurt as my ass opened farther and farther the deeper his penis penetrated. I felt it when the ridge of his head passed into me and his shaft began to plunge inside. He buried himself all the way in and stilled, staying there unmoving as my butthole clenched and unclenched around his girth.

Tane began to pull back out. It hurt, but it also felt...good. I reached back between us and pulled my ass cheeks apart, and he pushed back in. My vagina twinged in excitement. Tane's thrusts came excitedly, quickly, and he pounded my ass hard! I moved one hand from giving him better access inside me to rub my clit. I felt him in my backside, but it also put pressure on my vagina inside me, pressuring that sweetest of spots. I rubbed myself quickly, and the intensity of everything exploded.

It was not just me exploding either. Tane's mouth was by my ear. I heard him take in a sharp breath, and his dick swelled, stretching my no-longer virgin ass wider. He spurted inside my ass. I rubbed faster.

"Don't you fucking stop!" I yelled at him. Rubbing faster as he pounded me harder, I came.

Afterward, I was lying next to him, my head resting on his chest, using his body as a pillow. He had an arm wrapped around my shoulders, holding me close. I never felt so safe before. It seemed like he would make all of the bad in the world go away.

I was vulnerable. And I was safe. That was weird.

"Tane?" I brushed one hand over his belly, and he twitched.

"Stop that!" he laughed from being tickled.

"I wonder what your secret is," I mused.

"What? What secret."

"Everyone has a secret," I told him. "I have a secret. It's a good one."

"Oh yeah?" he asked.

"Tell me your secret, and I'll tell you mine."

"I don't know," Tane said. "Your secret would have to be pretty damn good to trade for mine."

I turned my head and looked him in the eyes. "My secret is dangerous."

"I like danger." He smirked.

"Is yours dangerous?"

"Only if my mother finds out," he said.

I pinched his nipple. "Out with it."

"Ow, ow, ow! Not so hard!" he whined.

"Tell me!" I twisted.

"Ah!" he shouted.

Tane grabbed my hand and entwined his fingers with mine, keeping me from doing anything more with his nipple. I then help up my other hand and waved my fingers forward and back threateningly. "Tell me."

"Okay!" he said quickly. "Don't tell my mom! I'm begging you!"

I pinched my thumb and index finger together and said nothing.

"Yeah. I had had premarital sex."

"What?" I asked, confused.

"I've had sex before marriage."

"No shit."

He said, "I mean a lot of it. I'm kind of a man whore."

"And?" I wasn't sure what this was about. What was the secret?

"My family is Catholic. My mother would kill me. It's a sin."

I sat up from him, sitting cross-legged. "Are you telling me that people aren't supposed to have sex until they're married where you're from?"

"Well. Kind of. Sort of. It's more important for some. Others don't care. My mom does. Very much."

I laughed. "That's your secret? I thought you stabbed a man to death and left his body somewhere."

"That would be a good story," he said. "But no. I'm pretty boring. I just like sex. And I suppose I'm kind of a porn addict too."

"Porn?"

"Videos of people having sex."

"I know what videos are. There are ones of people having sex?" I was intrigued.

"Yeah. Probably more of that than even cat videos," he said. "And I realize that makes no cultural sense to you." And he was right in that.

"How can your society be so sexual while also refraining from sex until marriage?"

"Like I said, there are many different walks of life where I come from. People pretty much do as they please as long as it doesn't affect someone else."

"I don't understand."

"I guess you would just have to see it. So what's your deadly secret?"

I closed my eyes to find the courage to say what I had to. "You know how you asked if any of us can change into animals?"

"Yeah."

"I can."

"I thought you said nobody could."

I looked at him then. "I lied. I can. I change into a panther. That's how I hunt."

He looked at the boar, and probably for the first time really looked at the crushed skull, with the teeth punctures. "Oh shit!"

"And you remember what I said happened to the panthers?" I asked him.

"They were all killed."

"And any new panthers would be killed as well."

He sat up. "They would kill you?"

"That's why it's a secret."

"I bet."

I scooted closer to him. "I really like you."

"Huh? Yeah. I like you too."

I swallowed the lump in my throat. "I want to go with you."

We looked at each other in a moment of silence. Stunned for him, I would think. He was so beautiful. I never thought I would ever see a man like that. But I did. If I went with him, I wouldn't need to hide myself like I did here, and I would be free to see where our relationship could go. With this beautiful man and his wonderful cock. I knew then it wasn't love. He would be a great friend. But who knew? These kinds of things take time. It could become love. I might as well give it the time it needed.

"Are you sure?"

"Absolutely."

Chapter 8

I loved hunting rabbits! There was nothing more exhilarating. It was not because of any perceived danger. I mean, they're rabbits! It was because of how quick they were. Imagine trying to run down a cat. It was kind of like that. It took all of my speed and agility to catch those suckers. It really got the heart beating. And one is never enough. Once you pop one, you have to have another, and another. I hunted them all afternoon. By the time I was done, I had almost more than I could carry back to the village.

I strung them up, tied together by their hind legs. There were two clutches of them on opposite ends of a length of rope. I lifted it up and put it on my shoulder with a group of rabbits bouncing against my butt and the one in front against my thigh. In all, I was carrying ten of them back.

My abilities made me the best of the tribe's hunters in taking down rabbits. Since I was leaving, I figured I owed them one last big take. I liked to think I was so special that nobody could take my place, but they did fine before I was hunting, and they would do fine after I left. I had carved a place for me in the tribe, but it was more like I carved myself to fit the role. I changed for what they needed. A spirit like mine needed to stretch and test itself. I could never do that here.

I finally had convinced myself that I was doing the right thing.

I began the walk back to the village. When I was only a little ways out, I heard someone crying. Slowly, I headed toward the sound. I wanted to see who it was before I made any decision if I could help or not.

The first thing I saw was long, blond hair. That could only be one person on the whole of the island. She was sitting on a fallen tree; near the village but just far enough that she had some privacy. It was my princess, the teenage girl Gina.

I purposely made some noise as I walked up to her. She heard my coming and turned to look at me. She looked both terrified and despondent. I put the rabbits down and kneeled in front of her.

Placing my hands on her knees, I asked her, "What's wrong, sweetie?"

She just shook her head.

I sat next to her and took her hand in mine and put my other arm around her, pulling her to me. She did not try to resist. She leaned against me and cried harder.

"It's okay," I said to her. "Cry it out." And she did.

It was some time before she began to get a hold of herself. She sat back up and wiped the tears from her face. "Thanks."

I just smiled at her, giving her the warmest look I could manage.

"They're d...They're gone," she said.

"Oh." I knew instantly what she was taking about. Her parents had been executed already. In the tribe, parents' were not such a big thing. None of us knew who our fathers were, and mothers were not usually caregivers. Some of the women were wet-nurses. They coddled when needed, but mostly the whole tribe raised the young. Parents were a non-topic.

We knew our way was not the way of the rest of the world. That being true, I was not the right person to make this girl feel better, but there was nobody else.

"I could've saved them, but I didn't."

"It's not your fault."

"Don't say that to me!" she snapped. "I could have saved them, but I didn't even try. I was just so scared. How could I do what they wanted? I'm sure it's easy for people like you, but I wasn't raised for this. I was never supposed to do something like this. But I didn't even try. And now my parents are dead."

"Yeah, but..."

"I've always made bad decisions. I chose bad boyfriends. I'd rather spend all of my time away from my parents even if that meant being with people I didn't really like. I should have relished the time I had with them. I'll never get that time again. It's all because I'm just a stupid girl. God, how lame I sound."

"Enough of this pity!" I bit back at her. "You will always have choices to make. Maybe they won't be good choices, but they are the choices you have. Even a bad choice is fine as long as you embrace it and learn. Your choices have made you the person you are today. Now take those bad choices and make something good out of it."

I stood and picked up my rabbits and started to walk away. She said to me, "But what can I do now?"

I said to her without looking back, "If you want your choices to mean something, if you want to affect the rest of the world, you need to have power. Your choices affect you. Unless they affect others, you lack power. If you had power, you can dictate what choices are to be had. Without power, you are making decisions based on what others allow you to do. So without power, you don't have much for choices. There is always a choice, but that doesn't matter if you can't choose for others as well."

As I walked away from her, I really had to think if I was making the right decisions myself. I was going to leave everything behind, but like I said, I was merely choosing options the tribe gave me. I needed more options. I needed to make my own options. Maybe I couldn't find that in the new world I was going to, but I most surely did not have it on the island.

As for the choices I still had, I was not going to let time answer for me. Inaction is a choice just as much as action, but it is a choice that allows us to feel like we didn't have to make a stand for something. There is nothing worse than that. It's the coward's path, allowing circumstance to dictate our lives. I was not going to leave home and have so much unsaid to Lelei.

I dropped the rabbits off and went to find her.

Lelei was at one of the clothier's huts like normal. She smiled when she saw me and approached for a kiss. I didn't kiss her back. She noticed and took a step back, looking at me crossly. She shook her head. "No," she said sternly. "I figured this would happen. It's your reputation, you know? You always end it when everything is so good."

"I don't..."

"If you're going to do this, you owe me enough to not lie." She crossed her arms and just looked pissed. I would have thought she was the angriest scorned woman ever, if it wasn't for the tears welling up in her eyes.

"I'm sorry, Lelei."

"If you really were, you wouldn't leave me like this." She wiped her eyes and went back to crossing her arms. "So do I get a reason? Or is it just thanks for the good times and goodbye?"

"It's not like that."

"Then what's it like? Hm?"

I looked at her, uncertain of what to say.

"Well? Can you even say it to me?"

"I..."

She looked disgusted with me. "Let me help you out then. Is it because you've had some trauma that you cannot get over, and I make you so happy that you can't deal with it?"

"No," I choked out.

"At least say it," Lelei demanded.

"I really like you, but I don't see this going for the long haul. We might as well end it now instead of letting it go on longer and hurting more in the end."

100

"That's bullshit!" she yelled at me. "There's no reason this can't work."

"We want different things in life. It will create problems in the long run."

Lelei said, "And I'm willing to give us a chance to even get to those problems, so we can work through them. That's how relationships like this work. Didn't someone ever tell you?"

"I'm a broken person. I'll just make your life impossibly hard."

She cocked her head sideways as she looked at me. It was unnerving, like she was trying to see into my head and see my thoughts. "It's because you're a shape shifter."

My eyes have never been that wide before. I looked around us in utter terror, but nobody was nearby to hear. I faced her and said quietly, "I have no idea what you're talking about."

She looked incredulous. "I understand why you want to hide that. But I've seen it. You're beautiful as a panther too."

"Huh, how? How long have you known?"

"About a month now."

"And you didn't say anything?" I asked.

"You apparently didn't want to bring it up, and I wasn't going to push it. I figured you would mention it when you were ready. But I didn't think you would just leave me like this. Is this why you left the others after so little time?"

"Yes," I croaked out.

"It's okay." She smiled at me then, and it was breaking my heart. "You don't have to be afraid of me telling anyone. I haven't."

"So you know my secret."

"And I still want to be with you. I must love you. You know that right?" Lelei said.

"And what if I don't stay with you? Will you tell everyone then?"

She looked shocked immediately, and that gave way to being offended. "No. I wouldn't want anything bad to happen to you. Should we be worried about you? Are you going to turn your power against us to take over? I don't think you would do that."

"And if I did?"

"Then none of this would be necessary, would it? You wouldn't have to worry about someone finding out your secret. But seeing as I already have, can't you see that you can trust me? I never even told you that I knew."

"I guess I can trust you," I said.

"What do we do now?"

"You see, the problem is I have always lived my life to keep my secret hidden."

"That hasn't changed. The secret is just both of ours now," Lelei said.

"Yeah, I suppose it is, but it's not my only secret. I've found ambition outside of hiding."

Lelei said, "Have you now?" She smiled conspiratorially at me. "How I see this going down is you need to be in the Blessed. Make as many children as you can, but keep them close. It may take years for enough of them to be old enough to help, but you will be able to take over everything. I know you have power, but you can't take over the tribe by yourself. The first queen took control with her nine warriors."

I took a step back from her. "You want me to repeat the past?"

"Mother Goddess wants you to," she said to me. "That's why the power has come back. She gave it to you to fix the tribe."

"No, Lelei, that's not what I want. The tribe is fine. It's just that I'm not meant to be here."

The color drained from Lelei's face. "What are you going to do?"

"You already know my secret, so I suppose my other secret will be safe with you too." I swallowed before continuing, trying to find the nerve to speak. "I'm leaving."

"Leaving?"

"I'm leaving the island."

"How?" she asked.

"A ship is coming, and I'm catching a ride."

"You're really leaving?"

"Yeah," I replied.

"Take me with you."

"What? You can't be serious."

"I am. I want adventure just as much as you do."

I laughed. "Really?"

"Yeah."

"My decision still stands, about us I mean. I hope you realize."

Lelei reached forward and touched my face. "Well, we'll just have to see what happens."

I nodded to her. "Then let's see what happens."

Chapter 9

It was petty of me, I know, but I had to do it. The ship that was coming for us was going to meet us under the cover of night, near the lagoon. We would light a fire on the beach for them to see us. Near the lagoon. That's where I took Tane, to exactly where I had watched him fuck Emere. Petty, like I said, but I was going to claim him as mine there. He claimed me earlier, and now it was my turn.

I spent some time that day wondering if there was anybody I wanted to say goodbye to. There was no one though. I just had a lot of ex-lovers and no real friends. That's what happens when you keep people at a distance.

I wasn't truly sure if Lelei was among the exes now or not. I didn't have much need to cut her out of my life any more, but I didn't want anything set in stone. At least for a while. I had the whole world ahead of me. I would see where I ended up and who was there with me when I arrived.

I had a pack with a few articles of clothing with me, and a handful of trinkets to remind me of home. I thought about leaving all that behind, but I didn't want to just forget it all when I left. Maybe someday I would come back. I didn't want to think about that though. I didn't want to give myself an escape.

I was building the fire while Tane laid out a blanket for us to wait on. I got the fire going quickly, fueled from some random bits of wood I picked up on our walk out here. It was soon popping and cracking.

"I'm surprised you wanted to come," he said to me from where he sat on the blanket. I looked him over. He was wearing the clothes he came to the island in. It was a white shirt and jean pants with black sneakers.

"I'm full of surprises. What surprised me is that Lelei wanted to come."

"And where is she?"

"Lelei will be here before the ship shows up. She felt she needed to leave letters for friends, telling them why she is leaving. I don't think it's a good idea, but I figure it can't do any harm. She has a lot of friends anyway. Everyone likes her."

106

"She's so kind."

"Yes she is."

"And so are you."

"Don't start trying to flatter me now!"

"It's true," he insisted. "The both of you helped me out so much in the cookery. It's not going to be an issue now, but I don't think I would have made it in the tribe otherwise."

"It was an easy thing. No big deal."

"Taking down a boar is no big deal for you?"

I shrugged. "It's what I do. I hunt that which I want. And I always catch it!"

I got on my hands and knees and prowled toward him through the sand. When my hand landed on the blanket, I changed my eyes to the panther and locked him in a gaze. It was the most animalistic look I could make short of donning the panther's face.

"Uh." He sounded uncertain and leaned away from me.

"I catch everything I hunt," I reiterated. A growl rumbled from my throat, and I swear he almost ran right then. I wasn't going to give him the chance. I pounced at him, and fear actually showed in his wide eyes.

I held him down. Oh, he tried to fight me, but he couldn't break my grasp as my muscles took the raw strength of the panther to overpower him. He struggled, but he couldn't do anything. I licked my lips in excitement.

I pulled at the waist of his clothes, but they were buttoned tight. My fingernails grew, changing into claws. I ran them softly down his flat stomach, making gooseflesh. When my nails reached his pants, I curled the claws under the waistband and pulled. They were so sharp, they cut through the cloth, shredding it. I ran a claw down his pant leg, slicing it. I grabbed the bottom of his pant legs and pulled hard, removing them in a great flourish.

Naked, he stared at me. He was very much afraid, but he would get over that soon. I was sure of that. I crawled back up his now bare leg while I allowed my claws to change back to nails again, just longer than the stubs I usually had. I ran the nails up his skin, and he stiffened all over. Just not the area I was interested in.

Reaching forward, I grabbed his flaccid manhood. He jumped, but I think he was starting to realize what was happening here. I intended to show him what I would do for him, but it was just too limp. So I licked it, and a shiver coursed through him. I placed my lips around the head and sucked it deep into my mouth, all the way to the back of my throat.

I growled again, and the vibrations helped. I felt it beginning to swell and pull itself up. I pulled my mouth off of it and began to pump it in my fist. It grew harder and harder with my attentions. I beat it, up and down, stroking the shaft, and watched mesmerized at it grew. It stood up and grew wider and longer. Inches of length were discovered at it got excited, adding to my own excitement. I continued to pump my hand along its now considerable length.

It grew in girth as well, making my hand no longer able to close around it. It was magnificent! I licked the head of it, making it glossy with my spit. I felt it throbbing under my tongue and hand. He began to grunt in time with the throbbing. Was it too hard? Could that happen? Either way, I would need to do something to relieve the pressure he felt.

I pulled off my wrap and skirt then. Rubbing my naked body against his, I slid up him until I felt his hard cock push between by boobs. It was slippery with my spit. I snarled at him and grabbed my nipples, pinching them painfully wonderful and pushed my tits together around him. I slid up and down while watching his penis' head push out and then hide like a turtle. I licked it each time it came toward me before hiding back into my bosom.

But I had enough of this. It was my turn. I always get what I hunted! I slid up him again, biting his nipples on my way. I kissed his mouth before sitting up, straddling his waist. His cock rested between his body and my moist channel. I rubbed against it, sliding my sex along his. My juices dampened him even more, and he moaned. I moaned as well, relishing the feeling of it against my clit. But I wanted more!

I raised myself up on my knees and reached between us, grasping his manhood again. This time, instead of jerking it, I aimed it up, into me. I came down slowly, rubbing the head between my lips to find the spot. Once in place, I came down hard on it, filling me up to the top. It hurt, but the pain was sweet.

He cried out, but I bit my tongue to hold my own scream in. I was the predator here. Only prey screams when caught. Lowered back down on him, I gyrated my hips, pushing him in deeper. I rubbed hard against him, forcing every little bit of him inside me.

I reflected that I had wanted to take him away from Emere, and here we were, fucking where she had taken him, and in the same fashion. He was completely mine, maybe just for this moment, but mine nonetheless. And he fit into me perfectly and oh so deeply. He stretched me out as his cock was swollen so wide, so much more than the last time.

I rose up on my feet and placed my hands on his knees. Up on all fours, I leaned back, giving him a perfect view of my naked body. I humped him hard, moving my ass up and down, thrusting his dick inside my pussy. My toes curled, and I pounded against him harder and harder.

He moaned and screamed and twitched in pleasure. And it was all because of me. I felt so more powerful than I ever had before. I could do anything to him, and he would want all of it, relish every bit of me against him. My body was conducting, and he was the choir. I moved, and he sang.

He grabbed my hips and began thrusting, plunging into and out of me. It doubled the rhythm I had set, and I felt tingly all over my body. It was glorious.

He twisted then, rolling his hips and putting me on my back. I let him, seeing he was not trying to run anymore. He was fighting back against me, and that was what I wanted. That's the excitement any predator relished. He stayed inside of me the whole time, and as I laid there half on the sand and half on the blanket, he thrust his cock like a woodpecker, pounding into me so quickly I couldn't keep the scream in anymore.

I was just about to cum when he pulled out. He began to furiously rub his cock. He moaned loudly and squirted on my belly. His body relaxed, and he sat back on his haunches.

"I don't think so," I told him. "I get mine."

I rolled over on my hands and knees and wagged my ass toward him. "Fuck me! I'm not done!"

He rammed his manhood so hard into my I swear I was

going to split in two. It was like a spear into my neither regions. I shouted out, and I loved it. I felt something weird then. My panther tail was growing. That was new!

"What?" he questioned, but he did not worry much about it. He grasped my tail at its base and squeezed. Pleasure exploded, and I lost vision for a few seconds. I wrapped my tail around his forearm as he held onto it, pulling me back as he thrust forward.

I was so close! Why wasn't I cumming yet?

I released my tail from his arm and wrapped it around his body, using the muscles to pull him into me. He pounded hard against my ass. I lowered my boobs down to the sand and reached back between my legs with one hard. I grabbed his scrotum and slightly pulled on it.

I felt them tighten, and then I felt myself tighten. He exploded inside me, filling me with his warm spunk, and I came at the same time. We held ourselves there for an eternity, or at least it seemed like it. We were stuck in our coupling. My tail relaxed its hold on him, and the extra appendage went away. He pulled out of my moist canal, and I flopped on the sand, now entirely off of the blanket. He fell to the ground next to me.

We lay there, side by side, breathing heavily. The cool air blowing over the lagoon dried the sweat on our bodies and aired off our wet, dirty bits. I sat up and slipped my clothes back on. He had to get new clothes out of his sack as I had shredded them. That left him with the loincloth.

When we were fully clothed, Lelei came out of the forest and joined us. I knew she had been watching. It was in the way her own clothes looked hastily thrown on and her breathing was heavy, similar to ours.

I smiled at her. She smiled back.

A light shined over us then as Lelei reached us. It was not from the fire, nor was it lightening, starlight, or the moon. It was bright and focused. I looked out over the water and saw a ship. A smaller one was making its way toward us from the larger ship, and a spotlight was on its front.

All three of us jumped up and down so we could be easily seen.

And we were easily seen, especially with the spotlight on us near the fire. Coming out of the forest were numerous sisters. Many held spears, and they all looked angry. Someone must have found one of Lelei's letters much too early.

They charged toward us.

"Go!" I shouted at the two. "I'll slow them down. Swim out and get on that boat."

"No," Tane shouted. "I'm not leaving you to them."

I smiled at them. "They might be getting the drop on us,

but I think I have the bigger surprise for them. I don't intend to die tonight. I intend to fight."

I relaxed my mind, and I felt it snap. Lelei and Tane, not Tane any longer but Johnny, grew taller. My tail flickered in annoyance as they stood there, staring at me. I growled at them to run, and they finally did. I watched them hit the water before turning to my sisters.

They were not running at me anymore. They stood still. Uncertain and terrified. I chuckle-growled. I didn't want to hurt any one of them, but they were not going to stop us from finding this freedom Johnny spoke of. And I wasn't afraid anymore. They were going to see the real Asoese.

I ran at them, my paws sending up a spray of sand with each step. Some of my sisters were brave. Some held their ground. What I didn't think was how terrifying the stories of shape shifters were. Most of my sisters ran back into the woods screaming. I was the boogeyman come to life. I was the nightmare that they dared to not even speak of.

I felt powerful, though a little remorseful to become the thing they feared. But that was not my fault. I am who I am, and I was no longer going to not be true to myself.

While my animal instincts took over, I kept the presence of mind to not hunt them down, to clamp my jaws on those that ran, crushing their skulls like a boar. No. I had a job. I had to allow Tane and Lelei time to swim to the boat.

I focused on the most dangerous of my sisters. They were easy to spot. They all had rock fists. I bounded at the first one, teeth bared and claws extended. She swung her fist at me, but I merely swatted it away before coming down on her. My paws fell to her chest and knocked her down into the sand. She lay prone, knocked out. I jumped off of her and went to the next.

I was having fun, jumping from one to another, and more sisters ran. The fun ended though, after attacking the fifth one. A spear pierced me through the back. I fell to my side, gasping. I couldn't take a full breath! I rolled back to my feet and ran a distance away before turning back. It was hard to move. My limbs ached, and my head swam.

There were about twenty of them left, and they seemed more confident now that I had been hurt. After all, there was only one of me. I looked back to the boat. They were almost to it. I had to hold out just a little longer. I snarled and ran back to the fight.

They formed a half circle, but I wasn't going to do this their way. I changed direction and came at them from the side, hitting another one down. She fought back at me, trying to stab me with her spear. I bit deeply into her shoulder. She cried out and dropped the weapon.

Another came at me then. I jumped sideways, letting the spear pass through empty air. I lunged and grasped the shaft in my mouth. Biting down, I broke the spearhead off. Shaking my head back and forth vigorously, I pulled the shaft from her hand and tossed it into the sand. She looked at me for a second before running.

I took as deep a breath as I could and roared as loud as I could, screeching into the night. And that was that. Most of those that remained ran. Only a handful stayed, and they did not look like they wanted to continue the fight.

I checked on Tane and Lelei again. They were on the boat. About time! I turned and ran to the shore. When my first paw hit the water, I leapt forward, changing back into my human form midair. I was a naked girl when the water caught my body.

I swam, trying to make it to the boat as well. My left shoulder screamed at me as the water washed over my back. It was the wound. They don't go away when I change, and the salt water did not feel good on it. But still I swam. I pushed on through the pain. It was not much father to go to find freedom from the tribe.

I was losing blood, though I don't know how fast. That coupled with the pain made that swim the hardest thing I ever had to do. My body was rebelling against me, slowly shutting down and demanding rest. And then I saw the striped fin.

I was bleeding into the ocean, and that caught the attention of a shark. It was not coming directly at me. It was swimming around me, circling like a vulture. The boat was too far. I wouldn't make it. Not against a tiger shark. I laughed despite it all. A jaguar falling to a tiger shark. A little poetic, I thought.

I kept swimming forward, knowing the inevitable was coming.

It changed direction and swam right for me. I braced myself, wondering if this fear in my mind was what a boar felt when I attacked. I did not know what its teeth would feel like, but there was no escaping finding out at that point. I never thought I would go out a prey.

A spear flew past me from behind and struck the shark. It jerked sideways and turned away, swimming with its fin and the spear both breaking the surface. And like that, I was out of harm's way. I looked behind me and saw it was Emere who had saved me. She was swimming to me, using her webbed hands and feet to catch up.

"Let me go!" I shouted at her.

She drew near and began to tread water, keeping a little distance between us. She said, "Wherever you are going, live your life well. Just don't come back. They would kill you."

"You're not here to stop me?"

"No. You're my sister in many ways. In tribe. In blood. In fur. Go and live your life well." She then swam away from me, heading back to the beach.

I swam to the boat. Thankfully they came to me and pulled me on board. Tane wrapped a blanket around me while pressing a cloth to my back to stop the bleeding. Lelei was watching the beach as we moved farther away. She had tears on her cheeks. She was crying. I don't think she really thought about what she was doing until that moment. She realized she was leaving the island to never go back.

As for me, when I looked at the island I did not see a home I was leaving to never see again. I saw just the start of my life melting away as the future waited to greet me. I was not leaving home; I was heading home for the first time.

About the Author

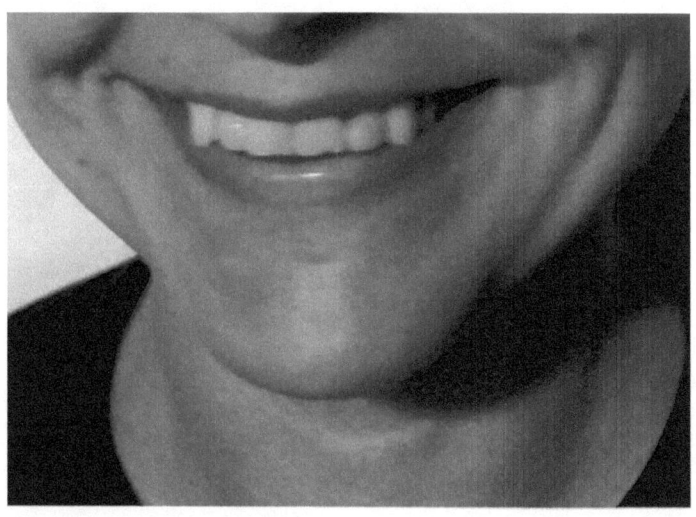

Despite her writings, Regina is a very private person, preferring a quiet evening at home over an adventurous night out. She does go out occasionally with a few friends and lives vicariously through them, eating up the stories of their sordid encounters.

She lives in Yankton, SD with her longtime boyfriend and their three cats. She has always been a writer, penning her first story in the fourth grade about two stupid rabbits. It was all downhill from there.